THE BOY
WHO BROUGHT
THE SEA

A NOVEL

ANNIE JAMES THOMAS

PRAISE FOR
THE BOY
WHO
BROUGHT
THE SEA

Published by Kimberly Pesaturo
Sturbridge, MA

Edited and cover design by Kimberly Pesaturo
Printed in the United States of America
FIRST EDITION 2024

Paperback ISBN 979-8-9914338-0-8
EBook ISBN 979-8-9914338-1-5

Fiction: Psychological

Fiction: Horror

For E, H, and my little Rosebud.

Contents

1

WINDOW ROCKS

Children passed outside, walking to the real schoolhouse with books under their arms, skipping and laughing while my face pressed against the cool bedroom pane. Behind them the channel surged, swollen with its late fall overflow. I didn't dare break my gaze. One boy caught my stare and threw a pebble at the window. It bounced where my face pressed. It was him, the same wicked boy that threw rocks into the channel.

I didn't blink.

"Take that, Violet!" His yell was muffled by the glass plate.

They never got our names right, no matter how many times I mouthed them. Violet was sickly, small, and blue: two rainbow shades off from her namesake.

The boy stopped and stared at me, dead in his tracks, like Papa used to say.

I didn't blink.

"Oh, children can be wicked. Fiona, step away from the window 'fore you catch cold." Nanny was remaking my bed.

I already made the bed. Tight corners, for a ten-year old.

Violet sat at the table.

Violet: less than ideal company.

A door slammed down the hall. Heavy boots passed our bedroom. Nanny pulled at the bedding, and I wanted to scream at her to let it go.

"Ms. Lally will be here soon, girls," Nanny said.

I withheld the scream.

"Please, Fiona, get your books and take your seat. Ms. Lally likes a timely start."

Violet coughed. I felt Nanny's eyebrows lower.

How do you feel someone's eyebrow lower? In the same way you'd feel the tighter pull of a bedsheet on a bed that's already made. That's how.

I don't remember if it was that day or a day like it when the chanting started, but the group of them sang it when they passed again in the afternoon. Worked it out during recess, I suspected, in the real school yard.

"Fiona and Violet, one left-hand, one right, they see to your soul, turn day into night."

"Fiona, no one's chanting," Violet said once.

But Violet never came near the window.

School yards weren't for us, Violet and me. We'd been in this house since the day we were born. Nanny and Ms. Lally were for us. Mama was for us. The waterway outside of our bedroom window shouldn't be ours, but I'd claimed it as my own. When Papa was here, he pointed out the window and told us that we were entitled to every one of our views; every cobblestone in our streets, every lamp that burned at night, every whitecap on the rushing foam.

I knew that Nanny heard the chanting. I knew that when Papa described the schoolhouse that was just out of view, I couldn't claim it because the wicked children already had. I knew that when you grow up only knowing the inside of a home, every detail you're afforded becomes critical information, like the color of Violet's face during sunrises and sunsets and how it changed with the weather.

This day featured a wrong shade of blue, even for Violet, with a coughing fit prompted during Ms. Lally's lesson on virtue.

"Virtue is our duty. There are four classic cardinal virtues, including wisdom, fortitude, temperance, and justice. Children, let's discuss this."

There's always the possibility that it was Violet who was wicked, or perhaps me. Nanny's face had been a bright shade of magenta when the Captain's boots got closest to our door. Maybe she was wicked, too, and maybe that's why we were all captives of this house.

"Fiona, under which cardinal virtue would you consider the act of patience?" asked Ms. Lally.

"The virtue of following Nanny's tidiness rules," I responded, to which I received my second time-out of the day.

In evening's safety while tucked into bed, I opened a fresh blank maroon journal and wrote. Much of my writing was untitled, so I always left the first page of my books clean.

"The devil is in the details," Papa would say, and my details were in the passages. Titles were mere deflectors of the truth.

That night's entry was dedicated to the boy on the street: 'If I had the power to turn days into nights, I would forward the clock years ahead so I could escape Mama, the Captain, Nanny, Ms. Lally, and Violet's creaking chair, tight sheets, mucus, philosophy, and all the stupid, wicked rules of this awful house that disallow me from recess and throwing my own rocks.'

The journal fit snuggly between the headboard and a nook in the wall. A stuffed fox toy fit snuggly between my elbow and chin. Aside from a wealth of memories, the fox was the last gift I had from Papa. The fox's name was Marlow. Marlow was my best friend. Despite being a jokester, Marlow liked to sing and had a shock of silver hair between two pointy ears.

I thought of the boy and reopened the journal.

'You're mine,' I wrote.

2

11:34 AND ALL IS NEVER WELL

Violet and I disagreed on many things, but our arguments were never really fair. She didn't have the stamina for them. I know how this sounds but outwitting her was far too easy. Her brain could focus on breathing or it could focus on thinking, but the two couldn't manifest together in the same space. You wouldn't want to hear the coughing, either. It wracked her body with fits. I swear, I felt it in my chest when she started up. It began with a small thrumming deep in my diaphragm, a wretched hum clawing its way up my lungs to the smaller bronchioles, then to the main bronchi, until it clung to my epiglottis and I was forced to clear my throat to be in her presence.

"Fiona," *cough.*

"What?" the thrumming began. "Is the time near?"

Cough. Cough. Cough cough cough cough cough.

"6 minutes away."

Infant fingernails scraped my bronchial tree. Can you imagine those thin little nails, begging for a trim while climbing their paper shards up your breathing tube?

"Could (*cough*) I (*cough cough*) have my (*cough*) blanket?"

I put the blanket over her shoulders, ran into the hall, pressed my back into the wood paneling and took a deep breath.

Another breath.

Another.

It's like staying under the bathtub water too long until your lungs become flames, and the only fire extinguisher is exploding through the surface for air.

Another.

My fingers pinked up and stopped tingling. When the coughing silenced, I crept back in. She couldn't be alone when it happened, and it happened every day that the Captain was here, at that precise time. I looked at the clock. We were a minute away. I swallowed hard and walked over to Violet. This would be Nanny's job on a Saturday, or Ms. Lally's job on weekdays. Sundays were my days.

Sundays were wicked.

What day is it today?

"I'm cold, Fiona," *cough*.

I tried to ignore her but couldn't. We'd been alone together in the house for far too long. The outside channel called to us both, though Violet wouldn't admit it. She wished for a schoolhouse with a real recess yard, and I knew because when I asked her in her sleep, she cried.

Placing my hands on either side of her arms, I rubbed up and down like Nanny and Ms. Lally did. Even through the blanket, Violet felt cold. Mama said that's what happens when you don't have it in you to get up and move around. Her body didn't make enough heat. Violet smelled like our bedroom, too. Or, our bedroom like her. I never knew which. The smell wasn't bad, maybe a bit stale like the back of the food pantry; Nanny swept everywhere but there. When I breathed Violet in close-range, my heart beat faster. I breathed harder, rubbed harder, until a flush raised to my face, arms, and chest.

"Ow, ow," she cried.

When the 11:34 cannon discharged from our roof with a massive explosion, its mental relief was like the cough Violet wished she could take. The poor girl stiffened, shaking in my arms like a bony baby bird.

"Maybe you can sing to her," Marlow said. "*When the home is good as gold...*"

I didn't sing. I smiled. I always smiled when the Captain fired.

"You forgot to co-co-cover my ears," Violet whimpered.

"You survived," I shrugged, picked up Marlow from the floor, and left Violet to her wheezing.

"If you can handle the cannon, she can handle the cannon. Twins are twins," Marlow said in his jingly voice.

"Try telling that to Mama!" I laughed and then Marlow laughed.

Turns out, 11:34 was my favorite number. Maybe it always had been because it was Violet's least favorite. We couldn't truly disagree over a number, but its representation. She'd never see ration and reason, that the Captain had duties whether on sea or shore. No; sickly Violet would only see emotion.

I'd asked Damon why the Captain fired the cannon at 11:34 each morning. We'd been lying in the courtyard. My head was on his chest and he smelled like fish.

"Oh, dear Fiona. When you're away at sea you can't fear drowning. But you do fear hell. When you flip and invert the number 11:34, what do see?"

He reached up and gently pushed on my eyelids with his fingertips.

"Stars," I said.

"Think harder," he insisted.

"Oh," I smiled, holding the image in my mind. "I see the word 'hell.'"

"Yes. You fire the cannon at 11:34. It's a warning to the devil. A declaration: *we will not meet today*."

"Does it work?" I asked.

"I think so. I'm alive, aren't I?"

I wanted to explain this to Violet, but the sad truth remained: when you're stuck in a house for every waking day of your life, does emotion become your rational reason?

3

ONE

There was no rational reason for my dearest Damon.

Papa said, "When two people are in the deepest love, the bond that forms makes you inseparable. Your hearts become one."

Damon was me and I was him.

4

STRING THEORY

Damon told me that our bond was called 'string theory.' It was a concept he made up to keep us connected.

"I know you made it up, because I'd recognize it if was real," I insisted.

"My sweet girl," he spoke with his breath. "Aren't we confident in our knowledge?"

"Yes," I nodded. "Very."

We were crouched down in the garden behind the courtyard's gate, risking punishment for being caught. My punishment would be bedroom confinement, but Damon risked the Captain's whip. I knew the trees would protect us, those pillars that stood watch over my queendom.

"String theory, Fi. Imagine a gentle knot tied to your arm."

"I don't like things tied to my arm," I said.

"I said it would be gentle," Damon laughed. He picked up my wrist and kissed the spot that visibly pulsed with blood. "I would insert it right here. Like a thin little fishhook threading into your vein."

I leaned my head back and closed my eyes as his lips worked their way up my inner arm.

"Harsh," I whispered, eyes closed.

He removed a knife from his pocket. With the flat side of the blade he pushed into my wrist until the skin indented, then pulled it away and kissed it again. "I'd never hurt you."

"String theory," I repeated. "You'll never hurt me."

"Never," he cleared his throat. "This point connects to an invisible string that cuts through space and time. On the other end, no matter where I am, the string is knotted to me. Right here."

He took my finger and placed it to a vein on his wrist. When I pressed my finger there, I felt his heartbeat, strong and steady.

"On second thought, I prefer to think my end connects here," I whispered, and lifted his hand to the center of my dress bodice. Pushing his palm inwards with the slightest force, I asked if he could feel my heartbeat.

He nodded.

"String theory, Fiona. For anytime I'm not with you but you need to feel me, place your hand on your heart."

He placed his finger to his wrist.

We'd never lose track of each other. Such was the promise contained within Damon's invisible rope.

"Remember, Fiona," Papa always said, "A promise made is a promise kept."

"Let's try it out," I squealed, running from Damon, ducking and dodging the unruly oak fingers branching from their aged and royal owners. They only tried to tickle me, those kingly pillars of wisdom. I stopped and rubbed my fingers over the leaf of a missus. She giggled.

"Come on, Damon! Find me! Tug the string!"

Nanny tugged the corner.

"Damon!"

I already made the bed.

"Damon!"

The string...

"...works beautifully, my love. You hide well." Breathless, he pulled me into his arms and buried his face into my hair. "I must return to the docks before I'm noticed gone. But first, here." His hand was on my heart. "Here, I stay, and here," he tapped his wrist, "are you."

Damon's voice carried on the wind as he blew back to the water, and I returned safely to bed, tucked in with the strictest precision by all the wooden hands.

5

THE PRECIOUS LADIES OF DINNER

Mama tolerated a few things, but not being late to dinner. She was a stern woman that spent her days quietly in the kitchen or her bedroom parlor. Mama was no Papa; she was not full of stories and could not spout math or tell us the history of the piano or coal tar or how electricity worked. I waited at the dining room threshold with my hands resting on Violet's wheeled chair.

Cold dinner caused a ripple on the watery household surface; the Captain became upset with Mama, Mama became upset with me, and I became upset with myself, risking taking it out on Violet. Papa would have been upset with no one and we would have laughed at a cold dinner, pretending we were picnicking along the snowy drifts of the Arctic tundra.

Each evening at half past four o'clock, the dinner bell rang, and I angled Violet's wheeled chair over the threshold. If the front wheels came down with force, I could not be blamed. Like all things too big for their own good, the house contained its imperfections. Papa would have adjusted the uneven floors. The Captain ignored them.

"Why do we wait for the dinner bell, Fiona? Just bring me in. Waiting seems silly," *cough. Cough cough.*

"Why do we do anything in life? That's the schedule of things." It was Mama's schedule.

Rrriiiinnnnnngggggg.

"Ooooh!" The front wheels hit, as I knew they would, as they always did. "My apologies, sister. This chair is so cumbersome, and the house not built for accommodation."

Marlow giggled from upstairs. I left him on the bed guarding my latest journal.

"Could you please wheel me to the carpet?" Violet's voice shook as her chair fought the floor.

"There's just so much more space to the bare floor. But, yes, I suppose, I could," I groaned while maneuvering the chair despite it hardly taking any effort.

"Much better. Thank you."

She was not thankful, not as thankful as she could have been. I pushed her into the table's empty space. Nanny watched from the far dining entrance. She was silent, but then swept into the room as if she hadn't been waiting at all.

"Please do sit, Fiona. Your mother will be in momentarily." Nanny picked up my left hand. "You're covered in graphite.

Next time, scrub before dinner. Always with these pencils, leaving them in your pockets so I find them in the wash."

Nanny was thin and gangly, with a lined face and long hound nose that could sniff out trouble. She adjusted the wheeled chair and placed a linen in Violet's lap. Violet's hands worked fine and were able to reach for the linen, despite being small and birdlike. I wanted to shout this at Nanny, but I was certain Nanny knew.

Then came the stomping. It was part of the ceremony.

He walked with the weight of water in his boots.

"Good evening, Captain," Nanny said from behind Violet. It was sing-songy nonsense.

"Good evening, Captain," we repeated. We were precious ladies with precious smiles batting precious eyelashes.

He whipped the chair from the table; Papa's chair.

"Hrumph." That voice: a plunger emerging from the suction of modern plumbing.

"It's the chains of all the men he's made walk the plank," Damon told me. "He carries it in his walk."

"How does that happen?" I asked.

"Captain's curse. When you accept the role of captain, you take on everything that comes with it. Can't have mutiny aboard a contained vessel. A good captain will not allow it, and the men will respect him for it."

"Seems rather harsh." All this talk of the Captain had been upsetting. I remember commandeering too much of something that night, or too much of something overtook me. That happened often when I was upset. Did I get into Mama's gin and forget? I told Damon, "seems raderer hash. Why can't he jus put them in the nest port when the ship stop?"

"Fiona," he laughed, "because a good captain shows no mercy."

"11:34 and all's never well," I slurred.

"No. 11:34 and all's well," he corrected.

"Thas what I said."

"Fiona. Fiona!" Mama chirped. "I said, are you enjoying the fish?"

"Oh, quite, Mama. It's very fresh." I took a big bite of my dinner in a show of gratitude.

"Is everything all right? You haven't spoken much this evening. Quite unlike you." Mama's food sat picked over, but her wine glass had been emptied, refilled, and emptied.

"Delicious, Mama. From the docks?" We only had the docks, but I had nothing else to say. I was careful to chew with my mouth closed.

"Yes, and a new delivery boy. Said he's from the docks. He brought the cart over after school today."

"What did he look like?"

I saw Nanny's glare and returned it with a precious smile.

"Fiona," Mama's voice was a storm warning, "inappropriate."

The wet tinny sound might have been Violet's giggle.

And then, I stared right at the Captain. I had no idea what made me do it. He stared right back. Cold, grey eyes and red, ruddy cheeks.

I held his glare.

Who blinked first?

Mama. Nanny. Violet.

But not me.

No way. I waited him out until he turned to Nanny. When I followed his eyes to her, she was the maroon of Mama's glass dregs.

"Heavens, I almost forgot the plum pudding," Mama stood with a clang of noise, breath, and heaving breast. Mama was pretty wicked if you ask me, because Mama never, ever, not once, forgot dessert when Papa was there.

6

OCTOPUS DIAMOND

It was deep night when I snuck to meet Damon in the courtyard. Deep night is that veiled time when ancient souls dwell in shadows and your mouth sticks together and your bladder wakes you up. One doesn't necessarily have to do with the others, but you can easily resolve two and ignore the third. Figure that out.

There was no signal that Damon arrived; no way to alert me that he was portside beside a rock thrown at the window. I spent those nights worried because it was all too easy to miss a ping at the pane in the shadow hours unless I was up and cursing Violet's wheezing.

Early in her sickness, she was sounds and smells. But in the later nights, she emitted heat; feverish, bed-bound and skin-sore. Violet was in constant progression. Her sickness oozed out of her when she breathed, from her lungs, her pores, and places we shall not discuss.

And always, I was bound to the house.

Mama had been pacing the widow's walk for two days, keeping lookout. Her heels clicked on the roof when she walked. I was the only one who felt their reverberation, and it was enough to shake the thoughts in my head.

In daylight, Violet praised the eleven o'clock hour because the Captain wasn't here to fire the cannon. I cursed 11:34 on the quiet days because I needed commotion to calm my noisy brain.

The ship pulled into port in late afternoon. I knew Mama would pace until the next day at least, or the following. The Captain never came directly to her and he never tried to hide the perfume on his filthy clothes when he arrived.

Please, don't feel sad for Mama.

She was no saint, either.

The Captain never came directly to Mama, but Damon came straight to me when the ship anchored.

"I have something for you, my dear!"

"What is it?" I held up his gift in the moonlight: a glittering black rock on a leather rope.

"An octopus diamond," he breathed into my ear.

I pulled away to get a better look at the rock. I let him lean in again, put his lips to my neck, and then my collarbone. I held the black rock in my hand, which tightened into a fist when his tongue traced its way slightly lower.

"You smell like fish."

"I thought you liked fish," he said.

"To eat," I laughed. Damon understood the part of my brain that thinks things incongruous with politeness, and I appreciated that. I wanted to tell him, but I chose not to spoil the moment.

"Then eat me," he said.

I ignored him. "I know all about the octopus, you know. From my studies."

"Fiona, are we still talking about this?" He straightened himself and grinned.

I stared at him; we all did. Me, the courtyard souls, the moonlight. We waited him out.

"Okay, I'll bite," he finally spoke. "What do you know about octopus?"

"Well, they have three hearts and blue blood. For starters."

"Okay."

"And they don't make diamonds."

"Ah, see that's where you're wrong," he smiled. He took the octopus rock from my hand and held it up in front of my face. "This one came from the belly of a herring. Legend says that when fish consume octopus ink under the right sea pressure, it can ferment in the stomach and become a diamond."

I grabbed it back. "A bezoar, you mean. Where can I find this legend?"

"A be-what?"

"A bezoar," I insisted.

"An octopus diamond, Fiona. It's a legend of the sea. Legends are stories that aren't contained in books." He rubbed his fingers across my lips. "You are smart, my bookish girl, but so naive. There is much of this world you'll never understand by being trapped in that house."

In the dim evening glimmer, it hit me. "Is this what you threw at my window? Had you been keeping it all this time? The one stone? You're a wicked, wicked person, Damon."

There's so much he never understood, and right then it whipped up a storm in my brain. I stepped away from him, white knuckling my herring ruminant.

"Thank you for my gift, Damon, but I hope our invisible string travels through stone walls tonight."

I fled back to the house before the ancients sucked the tears out of my eyes, pulled the cotton from my mouth, or poked me in the lower abdomen with their decrepit fingers.

Damon didn't say goodnight.

7

THINGS I
THINK I
KNOW

When I was ten years old, I made a list on a piece of loose paper. I shoved it under the mattress in early morning, and after lunch, discovered it gone.

There were no more lists after that.

Here's what I could recall from the list since I was left with no choice but to rewrite everything in my journal.

1. I did not believe that Violet and I were twins except that Mama forced us to celebrate our births on the same day. Each year, Violet grew sicker and I grew stronger. She was birdlike and bent, with that awful shade to her skin. If you said "boo" to her, she shook like a scared storybook puppy. My hands looked nothing like Violet's, and she wore clothes that I'd outgrown. You tell me if that sounds like two humans from the same sac.

2. As an infant, I drank milk from a bottle. She sucked the life from Mama like a leech. Phylum: *Annelida*. Subclass: *hirudinea*. Phylum: *Violet*. Subclass: *Teuling*. There are pho-

tographs to document this. I was once caught viewing them in the library and denied supper that evening. Mama said the photographs in that album were private, but the library downstairs wasn't private. It was apparently up to me to sort the nuances. Mama would never answer questions about things like leeches even if all household photographs were fair game.

3. Papa had a long nose and a beard that scratched my face. We understood science and logic together; I never understood why he left. There was no reason in it; therefore, it made no sense. It made me sad. I refused to believe his leaving contained any logic.

4. After Papa left, Mama cried enough tears to fill the channel. That's what Violet said. Violet had no idea how long, deep, or wide the channel was, so I told her never to speak such ignorance again. Papa would not have left us unless his life, or ours, depended on it. I could only logic, therefore, that the Captain threatened him right out of his own home. This would make sense considering how Mama let the Captain into her bedroom, dirty boots and all, while the rest of us were forbidden from wearing shoes on the carpet.

5. The Captain ate children for breakfast. (Maybe that one's not true, but he was a vile, evil man, and if I never saw him again, it would be too soon, e.g., see item number four.)

6. Asking Mama why Violet and I were bound to the house would result in her voice pitching toward the heavens, a hand striking her heaving breast, and forbidding me to never again speak of such nonsense.

7. Nanny told me the world was cruel and I should be grateful for such a "magnificent home" on a "beautiful waterway." Nanny, however, left the house on Sundays, which, according to reason, made Sundays her least favorite day. If I have ever before said that Nanny and I share no commonalities, I'm forced into mea culpa. Sundays were my least favorite of the days, as well.

On Sundays, I was alone with Violet. I've already explained this.

She moaned and I looked up from my writing.

"You're always at that window, Fiona. I wish you'd play a game with me."

"We played for over two hours, Violet. Don't your hands get tired? Or, your eyes?"

She saw the journal in my lap and said, "Don't your hands get tired?"

It might have only been a minute that I turned to gaze outside, my legs curled up on the cushioned seat, face absorbing the morning's slanted rays, but she stopped talking.

"Violet?"

Her head bobbed at the table. A line of drool clung to her lips, threatening to contaminate the wooden surface below. She could fall asleep faster than sleep itself. I got up and shifted her face back, severing the spit artery with her dress bib. She looked less uncomfortable, but with her, knowing was impossible. In that moment, there was no cough or wheeze, which were often her benchmarks of discomfort.

Sun-ray tendrils beckoned me back to the window. When I followed, they streamed closer. I closed my eyes and faced them, allowing them to caress me like a good mother's touch. First, they nestled my cheek, and next, when they tickled my lips, I opened my mouth to let the solar fingers poke around my oral cavity. They explored my incisors, cuspids, bicuspids, molars, -glossia, and mucosal surfaces. They kindly bypassed my gag reflex and traveled deep into the pit of my stomach.

'Come visit with us,' they gestured with long, ribbony pokes. This was an invitation to the outside world.

Would you have been an obscene guest and refused such a request?

Violet slept.

I looked to Marlow. He nodded, smiling his wonderful, mischievous foxy grin. He was humming a song to himself in the corner.

"Go," the wiry-haired animal whispered.

It was ten minutes past eleven in the morning. There was plenty of time to return before the cannon fired from the roof. I knew my path well. Left out of the door, follow the carpet runner to modulate sound, and pass three closed doors (guest rooms; never touched). Keep to the far wall before making a final descent to the right down the stairs into the main foyer, stop at the bottom to look left into the formal parlor, right into the library, and back, towards the dining room. If all was quiet, slip out the front door, duck below the windows and follow close to the house around to the back courtyard.

All was quiet that day. Mama rarely left her bedroom on Sundays and the Captain was preparing his disturbance of the peace.

Warm ribbony fingertips stirred in my belly. I opened the bedroom door and ran.

Once outside, crouched low, I whispered my hellos. "Good morning, *Quercus robur*, Sir Oak. Looking splendid as ever." He was so shy! You could pay him the complement, but rather best you didn't touch.

"And, you, *Betula pendula*, Lady Birch, don't you look lovely this morning." I ran my hands through her leaves. She liked the sensation, but you had to be gentle. Pads of your fingers only; no nails. The sun was warmer without the window barrier. A wind carried through, and I waited to feel the others, but sure enough, we were alone. Myself, the Lady and her Sir, and the dozen or so denizen trees that kept a steadfast watch. The wandering souls would return at night.

"Do you fear the cannon, too?" I asked, my voice carried upon a briny breeze. Maybe it would reach them, wherever the souls went in the bright day. I was quiet, fearful that a cyclone would whisk my words roof-ward to him. "Well, do you?" I paused, waiting for a response.

Do you know what silence is?

It's a deafening moment just before the Captain's bomb detonated. When 11:34 exploded in the courtyard, the sun-tendrils expelled themselves from my stomach, caught on my epiglottis, and left me gagging.

8

SNEAKING PAST THE WIDOW

I'll tell you this part, but you need to be really quiet.

No coughing, no clearing your throat. Don't write it down.

Talking like this, it all reminds me of that day. The silence it took, walking past her bedroom parlor, choking down the bile when I made one small misstep on the entire journey. It was a school day, but our studies were done. Fiona napped, and Nanny was sweeping the kitchen floor. Ms. Lally had gone to do what she did, whatever that was. The wicked children passed by the window, the group of them too intent on throwing rocks in the channel to pay me any attention.

My face left a grease mark on the bedroom window pane. I watched the children walk the entire length of the road, straining against the window until I heard it start to creak under the pressure of my face.

He looked back, right before they were all out of sight.

Saw me.

Stared.

Squinted.

Then he kept going, stumbling after the group to regain his spot. It was only a moment's hesitation before I decided to rush to the widow's walk to watch him go farther. Although the widow's walk was off limits, there wasn't much threat in "off limits" when leaving your home was forbidden. I hadn't been up there in a very long time and my previous punishment had been extra dish washing.

Time was crucial: the wicked children were getting away and they were getting away with him.

Barefoot, I ducked out of the bedroom and turned right, squishing along the hallway. I jumped the two stairs and dashed down the next hallway. I ran towards the alcove and up the spiral staircase. I slowed.

We can slow now, too, because I skipped the crucial part.

Have you figured out my mistake? I *looked left*.

When I passed Mama's bedroom, I looked left into the side-lights of her parlor door. I thought I was moving quickly, but I wasn't fast enough. What I saw when I looked left burned into my brain as if a giant hand held me down, and with a magnifier, let the sun shine through my open retina. Someone had roasted a pupillary insect in slow motion.

Mama was in her bedroom with the Captain.

I saw her and what she did. I saw what he did to her.

I saw how he did it and how familiar it was. It only took half of a second to see as I ran past her doorway. By the time I made it to the widow's walk and was in the direct afternoon glare of the rooftop, my eyeballs were completely scorched. Whether or not the boy was still in view, he was no longer visible.

9

NOTHING COMES FROM NOTHING

Papa used to joke about things like chickens and eggs, and then he'd invite Violet and me into a discussion of primordial soup. We gathered over Mama's large pot, peering in, ready to unravel the universe's deepest mysteries.

"This is the origin of life," he pronounced one day at our bedroom doorstep, holding the giant steel vessel.

Mama would never have given her kitchen pot over for Ms. Lally's teachings, not in 3.4 billion years.

Violet was so excited over what was in the pot that she almost fell out of her chair. Sunlight slanted in at an odd angle that day, and I recall the season as fall, although it could have easily been spring. Violet's skin glowed in a way that made her look almost translucent.

"Why, my dear Violet, you look radiant today," Papa's voice was stilted, but sincere. He was always sincere.

Papa told us we were beautiful, we were smart, we were talented, but I hated when he told her first or when he forgot to tell me.

Do you think I'm beautiful? Never mind. Beauty is irrelevant when you are smart.

I bound for the door and reached for the pot.

"In a moment, my dear Fiona. Be patient and the secrets of the universe shall be revealed."

He set the pot at our table, hand hovering above the lid like a magician ready to pull a rabbit from a hat.

As we marveled over sewing bits, scraps of bone, crumpled papers, and rocks, we learned about the hypothetical set of conditions upon which life sprang forth billions of years ago.

Papa picked up Marlow, asked how the fox could have come from this bowl of soup, and we discussed evolution. He held Marlow in one hand and formed the other into the shape of a bird.

"Picture different sets of theorists," he explained. "They can't always agree on one origin of a species or one simple means of evolution, but they tend toward agreement on this 'warm pool' theory. It's like our cooking pot, if you will. Now, I'll challenge you. We have the soup and its primordial components. What's missing from the picture?"

"The creator, " Violet said.

I nodded, dripping over every word Papa taught.

"And how can we introduce the creator concept to this equation?"

I never meant to knock over my chair, but lessons were the most exciting part of our days. You can see that, right?

"*Omne vivum ex vivo*," I shouted.

Papa laughed and hugged me, uprighting the chair. He did it without scolding. "That's correct, my creative, intelligent daughter."

There it was. What Violet took from an errant sun ray, I gained from demonstrating knowledge: Papa's admiration.

"And, my darling children, what does that mean?"

"All life comes from life," we spoke in unison, Violet and I.

We laughed together that day, pretending to dine on primordial soup from Mama's big pot, full on the wisdom and knowledge that something cannot simply spring forth from the vast nothingness of imagination.

10

A SPLIT LIP
IS A LIP
SPLIT

I forgot to finish the story about Violet. You remember, right? That day I escaped the house and ran into the courtyard's sunlight when the cannon shunned the devil? The day I wasn't there with her? I should have told you the rest.

When the cannon fired, the sun tendrils retreated from my stomach, catching on my gag reflex. It had been long enough since breakfast that my stomach refused to let go of much of anything onto the cobblestone walkway. I reversed my path to the front door and immediately ascended the stairs, but I wasn't fast enough. Mama was shrieking my name when my foot touched the landing. Instinct told me to run faster, but intuition froze me. When I slid into our bedroom, I was a lioness skulking an injured zebra.

I skulked until I saw the blood.

Blood trailed from the tabletop to the chair, the wood floor, Mama's hands, and ended at the bed sheets.

Mama was on her knees. Violet was rocking in bed. Mama was holding a cloth over Violet's face. Violet was trying to scream through it. The blood was zebra blood: *E. quagga. Equus quagga.*

Then, I was the hunter on the lion.

"Mama, no! Get off of her!"

The look Mama gave when she lifted the cloth was followed by Violet's pathetic whimper. "Me? Get off of her?" Mama was too calm when she spoke. Her words were slow and measured. "You weren't here."

"No," I spoke with caution, "no, I wasn't."

Violet: *whimper.*

"Well, where were you?" Mama whispered.

"The washroom," I lied. "I knew it was almost 11:34, but I had to go. It couldn't wait. So, I was in the washroom."

"No, Fiona. No, you weren't," she whispered.

Violet: *whimper.*

I became carrion, and Mama a crow circling the room. My own entrails dragged in invisible ropes across the floor. I pulled myself to the window.

"Get back here, Fiona," Mama's voice grew louder.

She picked up the line of guts and yanked me.

"You did this to her," she cried.

I bit my lip.

"She was alone and asleep at 11:34. Do you know what the sound of a cannon does to a sick, sleeping girl? Particularly one that is asleep in a wooden chair at a wooden table?"

Violet: *whimper*.

Mama put the cloth back to Violet's mouth, over Violet's mouth.

Whimper: *stifled*.

"Well, do you, Fiona?" Mama's voice escalated.

"Blood," the entrails murmured.

"Yes. A split lip. A nasty, broken lip. Blood. You won't leave her again at 11:34."

"No, Mama," I cried.

"No, Fiona, because you won't be leaving this room for a week." She threw the cloth into the pile of guts and shut the door on her way out.

We were left for dead, smeared on a slide. Two specimens, Violet and I, festering under Mama's microscope.

Split agar.

Fiona-side growth dominating Violet-side undergrowth. Or maybe, this time, the other way around.

11

BEDROOM DISSECTIONS

There was always too much time.

I'd over-explored the bedroom with all its cracks and fissures. If we started at the door and turned right, ornate white bookshelves overflowed by subject and genre. Books stacked for every season, reason and occasion. Cracked spines, dust covers, naked volumes, dog-eared pages, tomes of use and disuse. The area was carpeted with a worn Victorian. Those thread-bares counteracted the warped floors. Fine with me; it made for less sound. Less clues to Mama, the Captain, or whoever cared to listen in as to what I was doing.

In front of the bookshelves was our table with its chairs; it's where we "learned" with Ms. Lally. One thing I learned from Ms. Lally is that if you didn't mean something, you could put it in quotation marks with your fingers like *this*.

Next was a chalkboard and behind there, more shelving with school supplies. Science, math, samples and specimens. Then, my big window. Violet hated the sun. She burned through the pane in the summertime. Really, she burned if you accidentally aimed a candle in her direction. Under the window, there was a bench with a cushioned seat, and below that, games piled.

Our closet was a highlight, where you entered through the door closest to the window, walked the length along the adjoining wall, and exited out of a second door on the other side. Or, the other way, I suppose. Between the closet entry and exit doors were our wardrobes. Two, side by side. Violet's and mine. She wore my hand-me-down dresses because they fit her when I outgrew them.

On the last wall were our beds; each a twin like us. White headboards had floral wood carvings. Two beds for two sisters, separated by a hearth to keep us warm in the winters, drafty in the spring and fall, and serving no purpose in the summer except to echo thunderstorms. Paneling on the walls rose higher than my head, and ended at a point where white paper with faded roses began. At the very top, where wall met ceiling, was moulding unnecessary for Violet and myself. Crown, Mama called it. If she fancied herself a queen, make no mistake, we were not her princesses.

Then, a plain white ceiling. I'd asked Mama many times if I could paint us a mural of the sea on that bare expanse. A Scylla attacking a ship. Clouds that looked like wisps. Foamy waves.

"It would be our very own Sistine Chapel. But, on the channel."

"The Sistine Chapel is not the sea; it is the Book of Genesis and was brilliantly depicted by Michelangelo," Mama said. "You, Fiona, are not Michelangelo."

"Correct in your identification of person, Mama. And, we shall never discover the talent in my fingers if you never allow me to recreate The Odyssey over our bare paint."

"I can think of much better work for idle fingers, like sewing. Such a talented seamstress like yourself could be a big help around here."

And that was that. Until it was that again and again.

12

CIRCLES

As I began earlier, I retreated from Mama's doorway and the widow's walk, but I couldn't see anything. A radical blindness afflicted me. The carpet was thinner in the hall near Mama's room, where heavy boots had repeatedly squished its plush pile. I picked up the faint trail of Mama's perfume. I listened for Violet's mucousy cough and sniffed towards the bitter scent of our decaying bedroom. All were compass points on my dial, and I had to orient north. Or south. Or, just steady the spinning hands.

How long should it take for burned retinas to heal?

Ms. Lally didn't know the answer to that when I asked her the next day. She knew about things like Dante's *Inferno*.

"Ms. Lally, this is a serious medical question. I may lose complete use of my eyes."

"Fiona, I need you to ask a question pertinent to our studies," Ms. Lally responded.

"Okay, fine. Did you know that poem is about Dante's journey through the nine circles of H-E-L-L?"

"Thank you for spelling it, Fiona, and yes, of course I know what it's about. I taught it to you."

"Which circle is your favorite?" I asked.

"None of them. Why would you ask such nonsense?"

"That's not nonsense! You said yourself you love Dante! Why wouldn't you have a favorite circle? Everyone has a favorite circle. Violet, which one's yours?"

"Limbo," *cough*.

"See? Even Violet has a favorite." I looked over at my fox. "Marlow says his is lust."

"Who's Marlow?" Violet asked.

I ignored her ridiculous question. Everyone knew Marlow. I patted him between his ears on his silvery tuft of hair.

"Anyway, Marlow likes lust. Just like Mama and the Captain," I explained.

Ms. Lally turned that same shade of magenta I'd seen on Nanny many times before and told me to go take a time-out in the closet.

The boy walked by my window earlier that morning when I was using a magnifying glass to stare outside, trying to observe the sun's surface.

"Did it suddenly get very dark in here?" I asked Violet after turning from the window back into our bedroom.

"It looks the same to me."

Violet was a shadowy figure at our table. I got close to her face and made a show of opening my eyes wide. "Did you turn down the brightness of the sun?"

"You are so weird, Fiona."

"You smell funny."

"Leave me alone, Fiona."

You know where the boy kept showing up after that day? Behind my eyelids. An after-image. A fraudulent fiery outline: the eighth circle.

After my time-out, Ms. Lally instructed us to place our books on the table. Violet politely bookmarked her page with a soft leather marker.

"You're aggressive with your pages," she accused me without pointing a finger, but she was right. As much as I loved spines, I bent them like contortionists.

The hallway clock chimed a single bell to indicate half-past eleven. We neared my favorite time.

"Come, come, child."

Ms. Lally busied herself placing the blanket over Violet's shoulders and I stood up, wandering to the window. The streets below were empty of the wicked children. Water flowing through the channel wakened a familiar feeling.

"Ms. Lally, I need a moment."

"Hurry up, please, Fiona. I'd like to finish this Macbeth act before lunch."

"I thought we were discussing Dante."

"You were discussing Dante, Fiona," Ms. Lally replied. "We are discussing the Weird Sisters and their resemblance to the Fates of classical mythology."

Her last statement produced such a hearty laugh within me that I struggled to make it to the washroom without incident. I required no lessons on weird sisters.

The house shook while I was rinsing my hands.

Ms. Lally started, "Fiona, we began physics while you were dilly-dallying. Please pay attention. One train leaves Prague traveling 35 miles per kilometer. A second train..."

"Wait! I've heard this one before. I know the punchline." I didn't mean to knock the chair backwards, but excitement was such a rare bird.

"Ow!" Violet squawked, placing her tiny, bony skeleton fingers to her lips.

"Fiona! Look what you've done!" Ms. Lally's arms were around Violet faster than I could twitch my eyeballs.

I had scraped her with my fingernail when I waved my arms. Mid-flail, I felt it catch on her sandpapery pout. A spot of bluish-purple bubbled on her lip.

"I'm sorry, Vi," I offered and picked up my chair, a fallen soldier. I death-marched to the window. "Out, damned spot," I whispered at Violet's lip.

"*Out, damned spot, you don't belong, now grab a washcloth and sing a song!*" Marlow lilted from his spot on the bed.

I shot him a warning look.

Violet sobbed in Ms. Lally's arms. Mama always said Violet's pain sensors weren't right, and my poor, sad sister felt things harder and worse than the rest of us. Mama didn't know how hard it was to listen to Violet's breathing day after day.

"What do you have to say for yourself, Fiona?" Ms. Lally demanded.

After fogging up a window with my breath and rubbing the basics of a physics calculation into the grime, I said, "If one train leaves a Prague platform at 11:33 a.m. and a second train leaves the next Prague platform at 11:35 a.m. and only hell stands between the two trains, which one do you take to your final destination?"

"Fiona! Physics is not the problem," Ms. Lally argued.

"True! It's more a problem of philosophy," I said.

"I mean, what do you have to say to Violet?"

"Ms. Lally, with all due respect, I've already apologized. I thought we'd moved back to the lesson. What say you, Violet? Think I can sit at the table? Carry on with the train routes? I'll try to keep my excitement to a minimum."

"Yes, mmmhmmm. It's fine. I'm all right. Please, Fiona, sit, and for once, try to behave."

"What was that?" I repeated.

Ms. Lally's eyes bulged in a way that made my palms itch to reach and catch them should they pop out and fly in my direction.

"Ysmmmm," Violet murmured. "You can sit."

I sat and looked in her tinted face, into her sunken, sickly eyes.

"For once? Behave for once?"

"Yes." Violet's voice barely registered above a whisper. I sensed heat rise in my own cheeks.

"Vi? What are you implying?"

"Fiona. Please, not now. Lessons," *whisper-whispery-whisper*.

Ms. Lally's head bobbed back and forth like a court ball. Hand cupped to my ear, I ask Violet to repeat herself. "Is it your lip that's the issue?"

"11:33," she whispered, barely audible.

"What?" I asserted.

"I'd take the 11:33," she said a little louder.

My shoulders relaxed then. No one seemed to notice the clouds that had arrived until they broke in that moment and sun again streamed through the window. Ms. Lally's lungs audibly expelled all the gaseous breath onto which she'd been holding. I leaned in closer to Violet's face. Her scent was stronger there.

"Why?" I demanded.

"To leave the area near hell faster."

"Yes." Of course, that would be her train.

"And you'd take the 11:35."

"Yes."

"Why?" she whispered.

I looked straight in her little purpled eyes and smiled. "Oh, Violet. If you think the devil lives between two trains, you don't understand physics at all."

13

RIPPED
SEAMS

I thought Ms. Lally would have chosen gluttony, judging by her diameter factored by pi, but no, she never revealed her favorite circle of hell. She damned me to time-out through the alternative side of the closet and I was forced to enter through the left. Everything about that morning was going poorly, but I was committed to scientific examination of this misstep.

Thus, finding myself pushing through rows of outgrown dresses awaiting their turn with Violet, I saw it for the first time. It was hard to control my irritation in that moment, after years of right-sided closet entry; my dominant side. Right was always the side to "be" on. It was the side that I could control when I sped too fast and braked too quickly, running from no one in particular, and certainly not Violet. Violet, well, she was an implication of everything that was wrong; a human embodiment of incorrect.

A good scientist with an eye for hypothesis would nullify what I saw as a break in the wall, and on further inspection, a break in the wall that could be alternately designated as a hidden door. A three-centimeter-deep divergent seam emerged from the paneling, visible upon entry from "Violet's side." I grew nauseated that I had not been on the receiving end of a massive secret hiding in my own closet after all those years. I sat on the closet floor, cross-legged, and huffed before standing and pushing aside a row of dresses, trying to anchor my fingertips on the wall's bulging gap. It was hard to gain the correct purchase on the panel, which seemed to have warped and sagged with the house over ages of disuse.

Eyes watched me from the closet's corner; small, trusting eyes. I smiled at Marlow, who smiled back.

"You found it," he giggled.

"You knew?" I couldn't hide my surprise.

Marlow skulked away.

Using my feet to sturdy myself against some shelving, I pitched back and pulled. The principles of force, energy, and momentum interplayed until I tore the panel clean off the wall, fell, and created a whole bunch of unintended noise. I leaned my head out of the right-hand side. My side.

"I'm fine."

"Thank you, Fiona," Ms. Lally said. "Now, please stay in there until I ask you to come out."

"I'm fine, Violet."

"No one cares, Fiona."

"Ms. Lally cares."

"Back in the closet, please."

It was fine. I had work to do. The rectangle I'd opened was about thigh-high and as wide as a small chair: plenty big for me to crawl into, but a few feet in, I realized I entered a very dark space. I crawled forward and smacked my knees on a hard surface.

Have I told you I was perpetually black and blue back then? Here's a good example of how I acquired the bruises. Not like Violet and her natural hue. Mine were from honest work and exploration.

Feeling around, I realized I hit a narrow step. And another. And another. I couldn't go back for a light source so I had to use my non-ocular senses. When I succumbed to being a blind scientist, I turned a corner and looked up to see dust motes streaming in through a beam from a high window; an octagonal window in alternating red and blue panes. It was a window I recognized, one that sat right below the widow's walk.

I understood where I was.

The house—my entire world—held a secret from me for all these years, and I only then discovered it. I was sick in that moment, but also... something else. Bile rose in my throat and I swallowed it down. My fingertips grew numb. One minute I could breathe, and the next minute, I was some shadow version of Violet. Everything I ever knew was entirely wrong.

I had found secret stairs that accessed our attic.

There was something else about the octagonal window. If the one I was staring at was red and blue, then, a second, its twin, sat across the attic in alternating yellow and green panes. I remembered this window, as if yanked like an errant hair from my remote childhood memories with a pair of tweezers. This other entrance was not hidden, but it was forbidden and off-limits to me.

Do I even need to tell you where it was?

The other entrance was in Mama's bedroom.

As my world crashed into darkness, it also grew, grew, grew into light.

14

COCHLEAR
VIBRATIONS

Echolocation: the process of ringing the front door bell, transmitting vibrational frequencies to the cochlea of my inner ear, followed by me running to the stairway and stopping short of the descent. Ms. Lally would have cited the definition as wildly inaccurate. I can imagine her voice: "Fiona, the echolocation was the bell setting off its chime." My running was the response; I was a speeding mammal in an air tank.

"You're not a porpoise, Fiona."

I wasn't a dolphin, either. Although, I remember once reading that half of a dolphin's brain stays awake while they sleep so they can continue to breathe, and in that way, I resembled dolphins more closely than Violet did. But you sent a signal into our house. That part was true.

"Who are you?" I heard Mama ask, despite the fish cart outside that I could see from the upstairs landing.

I couldn't hear the response or the next question she asked. She blocked you and absorbed your waves. Kept them all for herself. Mama was always so selfish.

Then Mama shifted her weight and your response flooded my auditory canals.

"Slipped on some dock rot, ma'am. Broke his leg. Can't drive the cart for the time being. I'm a temporary replacement—the new day man until he recovers."

When your words zapped my body, I had to wonder if I had cochlea in places other than my ears.

I stared at you. Did you see me through the bannister rails? Could you feel my heartbeat trying to echolocate you, too? That's when I realized it, you know. Window rocks. Wicked children. Nasty rhymes. Unblinking. Vibrational window panes. You were a boy, pretending to be a man. All the versions of you were standing in the doorway of my house, selling fish to Mama. And then there was me. About six meters away and thirteen stairs up, swirling in a sea of sound waves, feeling like I was caught in an acoustic undertow.

15

SOUND OR
SILENCE

Dust motes. Mites? Mutes. *In silenzio!* Millions of mute mites streamed in silent single file through a daylight beam and threatened to sever my head from my body.

I ducked, dodged, and dashed. I was a ballerina in a bank heist. Can you picture it?

Maneuvering my way across creaking, sloping floor boards kicked up dust, dander, and filth. I avoided the threatening blade of light, breathing in every third necessary time. I'd put myself back in time-out for spilling lunch's fish stew on fresh linens, then loudly exclaiming that we needed an emergency fish delivery. I needed to get back to my attic exploration.

"Stop. What are those?" My own voice fell flat in the dead attic space, approaching the red and green octagonal window at the top of the stairs. I spoke the words, but the sound I made carried no echo, as if buffered by piles upon piles of—

"—all that gorgeous paper!" I shrieked in happiness.

I exhaled and pirouetted at the thought that millions of undiscovered words awaited me. Leather-bound journals with turned-out spines were piled high and as far as the light motes revealed. I discovered a library of unwanted pages left to die in the heat, cold, and every temperature in between. I reached for these riches, my fingers extended, calling them out from their depths and casting away other attic shadows.

This was the day for books. I twitched at the knowledge waiting in the pages. In all my years, I thought I'd uncovered every bit of information in this house, but here were dozens of books waiting to be read.

The souls watched from the little octagonal window. In daylight! It was as if they knew what I found or were in on the surprise. Although I'd spun in a hurry, I couldn't catch them. They always hid so fast.

The attic was dark, but I could make out each individual journal staring at me, yearning to be touched after years of neglect. If books had fingers, these were seeking to interlace theirs with mine.

Picking up a single volume, I dusted it off and held it against my cheek. My mouth released its tension into a round "O" shape.

Does noise make any sound in the absence of echo?

I was a girl in the garnet city, with books as sparkling jewels floor to ceiling, ready to be unearthed and draped over my body.

You want to know what the books were.

Of course you do. Anyone would.

I dove in like a diver above water.

16

THINGS THAT TIME BROUGHT MAMA

It was 11:33 in the morning and Violet was napping. Did your heart just skip a beat? Ha! There was no cannon that day. The Captain was away sailing uncharted waters or gutting men or ordering fish to raise the mast or something like that.

I could never help myself from standing over her bed when the long arm on the clock struck twenty-six minutes to noon. Leaning in near her bluish face, I held my breath and silently crashed my hands together mimicking a giant explosion.

"KAPOOOOOOOOWWW," I never said out loud.

She never flinched.

Nanny was downstairs with Ms. Lally, and Mama was preparing lunch. I pictured Ms. Lally picking at Mama's food while Nanny swept at the droppings.

KAPOOOOOOOOWWW.

There was a single stained pine board on our bedroom floor that made a good tight rope, but I could only balance on it for so long before the invisible crowd's applause died out. I itched to get some non-Violet air and a new audience.

Maybe the souls were out midday.

Likely not.

Mama's bedroom window faced the courtyard.

I dared not go.

Maybe only for a minute.

The carpet squished under my toes. It was so decadent to walk barefoot in the hallway. Nothing like splintering your soles on our threadbare rugs; no, that was like shuffling your feet across the unshaven faces of men for whom the hallway carpet was intended. Dirty men. Seafaring men like the Captain. Men that never smelled worthy of the pile. Or of Mama.

Her door was cracked. Not broken, but open. Words are funny. Ms. Lally often failed to see the humor in words and it resulted in many time-outs.

Mama's room smelled of burned smokey spice layered on sage and perfume. I knew I didn't have much time, but I wanted to see.

As soon as I walked into Mama's haven, the souls were all but forgotten. Her dressing table was first. I picked up a plain silver tin and opened it, tipping cards into my hands. These were not playing cards, but picture cards. Cards with swords, with priests, cards with ladies and men, and five-pointed stars in circles. There were illustrated cards in muted colors, flexible cards that had been used but not frayed. I put them back in their tin and rubbed my hands on my dress, removing their touch.

Next, I ran Mama's ivory comb through my unbraided hair. Stringy hair upset Nanny, but Nanny would not be upset that day, not after the comb.

Lifting the dressing table's right-sided latch, I examined a row of necklaces laid side by side. There were modest jewels, some I recognized as being from the Captain, but others I'd never seen, at least not around Mama's neck. One, a black, iridescent stone stood out among the others. I picked it up and held it to the light.

"An octopus diamond," I whispered. The words caught in my throat, and at once, it was as if the eyes of transient strangers were all watching me hold this treasure.

"You should put it back," Marlow said from somewhere deep in our bedroom. "You know what happens when you're bad."

Slowly, I placed the stone, lowered the table's cover, and turned in the chair. I expected to meet the eyes of pin-prickly onlookers.

Saw no one.

Exhaled.

The room itself began to pull me under and I knew my time had expired. Woozy, I slipped out and back down the hall. There was more to find, but I left those adventures for another time.

17

THE GARDEN'S STICKY FINGERS

For all the times I tried to catch them, the souls catching me was something of a frightening experience. It was like walking into a spider web.

"I see you all decided to make an appearance," I whispered, as their tangled, fingery strands held fast and sticky around me.

They were strings of beady sweat trying to keep me from reaching Damon in the garden. I pushed against them. They smelled dank and unwashed, like old plumbing. We were older then, Damon and I, older than when I'd found the attic or when I'd first discovered Mama's diamond. I worried less about what anyone thought or saw or did. I still hated the Captain.

"Dooooon't sppppeaaaakkkk," sulfurous voices wafted into my nostrils and hisses of, "dooon't tellllll," seeded my ears.

Damon waited by the far gate, away from any window's prying eyes. Although I worried less, the house was always on guard. The house still held Violet. My slippers unstuck themselves from courtyard molasses, but slowly, like I was peeling the old wallpaper from inside the closet.

"Wait," I whispered, "I'm coming." *Peel-stick-peel-stick-peel*.

"I can see you, you know."

I glared at him.

"You're walking awfully slow, Fiona."

"Keep your voice down, Damon."

"I'm whispering," he laughed.

"Nnnnooooooo," they all hissed.

"Let go of me," I pleaded, louder, and pushed against the wet smelly strings.

"Who are you talking to?" he asked.

"Them!" I gestured around me. Wildly, flapping, flailing, my arms indicating the air around my head. The souls were everywhere, holding on to me.

"Fiona, please, stay calm." He stood by the gate, blending into the darkness.

"I would if they'd let... go!" My voice rose higher.

"Come here, you."

When Damon reached out his arms, the sticky tentacle webs released their hold. I'm not sure if they gave me up, heard my admonishment, or trusted Damon. When he took possession, he rolled me into a hug. Our bodies lined up in a way that made complete sense.

Breasts to chest. Hips aligning. Legs intertwined. My head tilted up roughly forty-five degrees, and his tilted down forty-five degrees, locking our lips at the midpoint of the hypotenuse. When he ran his fingers through my hair, his hand caught in a tangle and pulled my head back, undoing our perfect triangle, but opening up my neck. His lips moved down, and their wet softness stayed with my pulsing carotid. The kiss was everything like Mama's hidden books said it was supposed to be.

Yes.

I'd found those books on another adventure.

Retinas on retinas on retinas. Damon pulled his hands from hips, his lips from my skin, and his fingers touched my mouth, brushing me like tiny feathers. I pushed his hands in, like dinner. Like he was food to eat. Chicken bones to be sucked dry.

"Oooh, Fiona," he moaned.

I looked at him. His eyes were closed and his mouth contorted into something that looked like pain, but that moan sounded nothing like it. Nothing at all.

Noise; visuals; touch and heat; bodily alignment.

"Mum me," I mumbled. I took his fingers from me mouth, and wiped the line of spit with my sleeve. "Touch me."

We sat on the cobblestones. Despite the darkness, his glistening fingers found their way, and together we rocked like a ship tossing in a storm. Rocked for a long time, but maybe only a minute. Sea-time is nothing like land time, you know. The two are entirely different.

He kissed me to muffle the noise. The sea took me, and I lost myself to the undertow. When the waves broke, I slid away and whispered my goodbyes.

"Fiona!" he whispered as loud as a whisper could be. "Fiona!"

"I'll come find you tomorrow night, Damon."

The souls were happy to have me back. Relieved at my good fortune. A few of them pulsed alongside me. I looked back at Damon and blew him a kiss. But, he only stood, one hand in his hair, one on his hip, his face twisted.

His whole face contorted. I recoiled as the Captain flashed in his features.

"No!" I shouted. "Please, Damon, no!"

And then, Damon's face was his own again, with Damon's lips mouthing words. Although I could not hear them, I knew they asked, "What are you doing? Why are you leaving? What just happened?"

Silly Damon. What just happened was ecstasy. Wasn't that obvious?

18

THE MAN WHO BUILT WORLDS

I don't know if the sound that woke me came from the hearth, Violet, or a dream, but I was sticky with sweat from my neck down to the backs of my knees. Evil men swarmed me in the night and one strong hand reached through the tangle to pull me to safety. I knew every vein on that hand as it glowed like a slice of moonlight through the window. Violet slept with her cawing snores. The call slipped past my lips before I was able to catch it and reel it back.

"Papa?"

My voice caught in the spiderweb between sleep and awake, the paternal arachnid crocheting some wisp of a gossamer dream.

Papa.

The word landed upright on the floor. I watched it move on all eight legs with an irregular quickness, straight into the cold fireplace.

And then it was gone.

The hallway clock rang twice. I sat up from my bed, pulled a blanket around my shoulders, and moved to the window seat. Below, the channel surged with the spring overflow, showing off in the brilliantly silent night. Hot exhale on the window pane, enough to forge a spider with my finger, bit me back with the sharpness of my midnight breath.

Papa: the man who built worlds.

You know, Mama wasn't so mean when Papa was around. He'd read with me for hours, and I didn't mind Violet listening in. Violet wasn't so much of a nuisance when Papa was at the helm of our books. Papa taught me how to hold a pencil and make worlds of my own in journals. The American frontier was won with Papa and our shotguns.

"Here, hold your fingers like this." Pointer out, thumb up, three collapsed. "Now, tuck it in your pocket."

Violet could walk back then. Braced legs. We'd step apart ten counted paces until Papa yelled, "Draw!"

He'd take Violet by the shoulders and tenderly lean her to the side, gently shaking her as I blew her away in a fury of bullets.

"That's how the west was won," he'd tell us.

I'd hoot and holler, galloping around the room on an invisible trusty steed.

By the time Ms. Lally entered for our studies, we'd be poured over Papa's notes, his drawings, his diagrams, discerning the morality of shooting another human; arguing the meaning of a life; dissecting the validity of taking a land that did not belong to you.

I'm not even sure that it was Papa leaving us that made Mama so mean.

No.

The change in Mama was timed much closer with the Captain's arrival.

19

SMILING
GARNET
EYES

There was a morning sometime in my teen years in which I was an old fisherman, and Nanny a weary fish. I'd hooked an unmade bed on my line and cast the reel, the way men do along the channel. Nanny swam in and bit hard, yanking me tight and quick. Uneven bedding corners whet that sea bass' appetite and she almost drowned me, but I fought hard and made it safely to the dry closet, clearly the winner in the epic battle. Nanny's eyes bugged out of her head, gasping to breathe. A slammed door severed the line and I cast her back out to the oceanic expanse of dealing with Violet.

"Thirty minutes in time-out," she blubbered. "You know the rules of tidiness."

I found the passage in the wall again, easier to navigate now that my fingers had acquainted with the grooves on the wood purchase and my feet had been properly introduced to the stairs. Windows became clocks when the sun shown down through the trees, creating angular hands of time through stained glass. Time became the enemy against which I'd been pitted.

Sparkly sea motes swam through the soupy attic air, and I moved my arms with the current. The attic books called out.

"*Touch us,*" they sang in their angelic soprano voices. "*Crack our spines. Break us. Let us breaaattthhhheee.*"

If I looked them in their garnet eyes, I'd never get past, but when I opened my mouth to explain, the words wouldn't come. I was too deep underwater.

And here I was, thinking it was me that hooked Nanny.

The darkness thickened as I paddled forward.

"Evolution and religion can absolutely go hand in hand, Fiona," Papa smiled at me. "Today, we'll focus solely on evolution."

Papa never saw books as statements. He was a bigger picture. A picture window. If you looked at Papa, you weren't on the outside looking in, you were one of a myriad of glittering eyes searching the great wide expanse.

"I'll propose a theory," he said. "An underwater being starts as a single-celled organism. Over time, compressed time for the sake of argument, that organism transforms itself through generations. It senses its needs and environment and creates its own resiliency, adaptability, and flexibility."

"What about a creature that dwells in mud?"

I shot Violet a look, but she didn't back down.

Instead, he placed his arm around her shoulder. "Vi, that's an excellent thought. Please elaborate."

"I feel sad for those creatures. They must hate their lives."

"Oh, my sweet Violet-flower. Don't feel sad for mud dwellers. They've made the darkness their home."

"They like it there?" she asked, her eyes round with concern.

"It's where they've learned to breathe, eat, grow, and most importantly, adapt."

I swam deeper into the attic's recesses, ignoring the crying garnet eyes.

"But it's mud. There's nothing of value. No sunlight, nothing to play with, no places to explore," Violet insisted.

No windows. When the mud gets in your eyes, you're blind to the world around you.

He kissed her hair. "They'd never know what they were missing."

"But that is sad, Papa."

Papa's eyes changed in that moment. Not from his normal green to any other color, even if they lost a bit of their shine just then. They didn't change in shape or feature, and the tiny birthmark on the white of the left one stayed in its place. Instead, Papa's eyes shifted deep in the folds of his retinas, in the great depths of his irises. There are no other ways to describe what I saw, because I hadn't ever before seen anything quite like it. It was like watching the sky and seeing a shooting star for the first time, and only being able to tell someone that a light was trying to run far, far across the universe.

A week later, Papa left. He and Mama told us he was leaving for work, an extended trip, not that research was unusual for him. But this trip would be different, longer.

He first kissed Violet, and next, me. I handed him Marlow.

"Take care of these ladies," he whispered to the fox. "Even if all you do is hang back and watch, help them when they need it." Then, he winked at me. That wink, I knew, was to make sure I saw his eyes. I couldn't find relief in either of them.

When he leaned in for one last hug, he buried his face in my ear. "I know you know how to swim, my intelligent little dolphin. Make sure my sweet dove, Violet, flies, too."

Taking a breath, I choked, but it was enough to know.

The hair on my neck prickled. It was time to backstroke to the bedroom, but something was different then. Reaching up under my braids, I felt the ridges.

My gills were starting to take shape.

20

THE BIRDS

Once, a long time after Papa left, Mama sat with us. Nanny and Ms. Lally told us we were bound for a special day with Mama, so on giant paper Violet and I drew Victorian castles filled with pastry cremes and ribbons, candles and bows, and life-sized frog-men dressed in haberdasher finery holding the doors open, trumpeting Mama's arrival as we, the Ladies of the Bedroom, waited to welcome Mama into the splendid tea awaiting her.

"Your Mama picked out several books today, and is quite happy to join you girls and discuss them," Nanny announced.

As the day dragged on, frog men in finery dissolved into a Hieronymus Bosch bedroom-scape. I looked at Violet, who looked as though she might gag on her own excitement. Violet's tongue lolled when she smiled, and her bird-like hands clung so hard to her chair that any blood left in them had entirely drained, converting them from purple to complete white.

Nanny ignored Violet, finished her sweeping, and tugged at the corner of my made bed.

We never had Mama's undivided attention. Mama was always preoccupied with the Captain, or was out on the roof walk, her heels tapping like a woodpecker pecking away at the shingles.

Peck, peck, peck, peck. Pause. Turn. *Peck, peck, peck, peck.*

Not that day. That day, Mama was giving herself to us and we were to be on our best behavior.

I was dressed in the newest frock I'd found in my side of the closet, a blue satin dress that dusted the floor. In a show of gratitude, I hadn't even winced when Nanny plaited my hair.

"Awfully quiet today," she'd commented. "You're not catching ill, are you?"

"Why, Nanny," I'd told her, "I'm sick with a need to learn."

It sounded appropriate in my head, but Violet snorted as the words left my mouth, and sent herself into a coughing fit which made her gag, and then she'd accidentally spittled all over the front of her hand-me-down dress and had to be changed.

I awaited the punishment that never came.

Marlow and I dashed around the room, silently addressing Mr. and Mrs. Hieronymus Frog at either side of the large door, adjusting Mr. Frog's bowtie, as Mrs. Frog forgot to do, and shame on her for not paying attention to detail on such a big day.

The door almost smacked me in the face when it opened, and Mama appeared in its frame.

"Watch out!" Marlow giggled.

"Come on, girls," Nanny's hands were on my back, ushering me to our table. "Have a seat so you're nice an' prepared for today's lessons." I heard the tone in Nanny's voice register a higher octave than normal. Its usual bitterness was tainted with a sweetness that sounded like it would make you sick if you ate it.

"Mama!" Violet rasped.

"Good afternoon, darlings," Mama pecked into the room. She was dressed in all black; a simple outfit as usual with her bosom at the helm.

Her feet tapped their way to our table.

Ms. Lally appeared behind her with a stack of books and after a quick scan of the titles, I realized I hadn't recognized them.

"New books!" I yelled, although it felt a bit like a betrayal that she'd withheld such a precious commodity.

"Fiona! Indoor voice, please," Ms. Lally said.

I giggled, as if there were any other type of voice in that house.

Mama came to the table and Ms. Lally set down the books. Ms. Lally pulled a chair for Mama, who eyed the chair like a circling hawk before she sat.

I'd figured out what this was: a momentary Möbius strip. When I looked at Violet's claw-like fingers, blood-drained and gripping the seats, waiting for Mama to take a place that did not belong to her, she felt it, too. Nanny's face turned that familiar shade of magenta. Ms. Lally's forehead perspired.

If I could have used that moment to flex my new-found hawk wings, I would have flown far away in search of Papa, not resting until I returned him home safely in my beak.

"Squawk," Violet coughed. "Squawk, squawk, squawk," she sputtered. She was in agreement, explaining that we'd quietly perch until the moment was perfect.

No one moved until both Mama and Nanny approached the bony restless animal at the same time to clean her drooling chin. Nanny won and Mama tapped her way back to the chair.

My hawk belly grumbled.

Mama announced: "It's time for our lesson together, my darlings."

Violet and I locked eyes.

Then, we devoured her.

21

MAMA'S LESSONS

Despite being eaten that first time, Mama tried to teach us again, again, and again.

"Mama, what are we learning about?" Violet wobbled as she leaned forward, a line of spit hanging from her chin.

"Can you wipe her face?" Mama gestured to Ms. Lally, breaking an unwritten rule of the bedroom. We didn't point out Violet's flaws, we only took care of them.

I gasped at Mama's poor taste and took up the cloth myself.

It was winter then, and the morning had placed us all in a frost. If you were there in that moment, your eyeballs would have frozen wide open, too. When the shock of Mama's rudeness startled Violet, my sister's small purple spirit broke free from her chin and shattered like an icicle on the table below.

Although Ms. Lally never moved, I saw winter in her eyes, the coldness directed at Mama. My chest hurt for Ms. Lally, but only for a second. The ache left in a foggy breath when Mama turned open book pages and we all exhaled.

"Let's begin today with mathematics, shall we?"

"Yes!" I banged my leg under the table, the excitement rushing back into the room.

"Wonderful," Mama said.

She looked at the book and began to write on her paper.

"Mama, are we discussing Pythagoras today? Euclid? Euhler? Oh! I think Euhler is my favorite. Vi, who's your favorite? I get excited about Euhler because Papa once told us that the basis for his famous theorem was the calculation of an infinite number of sums, and I think anything in infinity is magical. It's beyond imagination." I had left Antarctica and was wrapped up in a world of imaginary units, bases of the natural algorithm, and was standing in the corner of the angle in radians.

When my excitement finally faded, I saw the magenta swell in the faces of grown-ups. Mama had crumbled the paper in front of her, but not before I saw this:

'Per-cents. X/100. 50/100 = 50%.'

"Mama, what's on your paper?"

Mama's look was permafrost and her words almost froze us out of the bedroom. "Nothing, Violet."

Everyone else around her grew hot. She, however, was un-meltable.

"Well, Mama? Is it Euler?" I asked.

"Children, I forgot I have other responsibilities today. Carry on with Ms. Lally. Oh, and someone please wipe her chin again."

She exited the room leaving her books and pages behind. The crumpled paper went with her.

Ms. Lally wasted no time. "Children, identify the Pythagorean Theorem."

Violet answered faster than I did, but only because my mind was elsewhere: "It's the relationship among three sides of a right triangle, defined by the sums of the areas of squares."

I was stuck on the fact that if a-squared plus b-squared equaled c-squared, it accounted for me, Violet and Papa. Poor Mama. She had no place in our equation and was beginning to figure that out.

22

HEADACHE

"Violet," I whispered. "Violet, wake up."

Despite being older then, Violet had a tendency to fall asleep in her wheeled chair like an overgrown infant.

"Violet," I touched her curled hand.

"Seven moons," she drooled.

"One moon," I corrected.

"What?" Her papery eyelids fluttered and she uprighted herself. "I was sleeping, Fi."

"Yes, but there's a man in the house."

"Papa?" She asked too suddenly which led to a coughing fit.

"Geez, Violet, no, and please relax. I hear his voice in the dining room. Take this."

The pack I placed on her lap contained our necessary spy supplies: a writing tablet, chalk, an old pair of glasses I'd found, binoculars, and a magnifying glass on a chain.

We wheeled to the edge of the stairs and listened over the bannister.

"Do not cough," I told her in my sternest voice.

Pack in hand, I padded barefoot down the stairs, leaving Violet at the landing.

When I looked back, her purple bird arms were reaching for the railing trying to pull her chair closer.

"No!" I mouthed as loudly as silence allowed, flailing my hands. "Stop!" I rushed back to her. "What are you doing?"

"If Mama has a new man, I want to see him."

"You're going to fall," I warned.

"I'm not," she insisted.

I was a candle with a flaming head and wanted to light her on fire. She should have stayed asleep and I should have adventured alone, but Papa's voice was alive in my head. *Help Violet fly...* I'd felt obliged.

"Here." I tossed the binoculars into her lap. "Use these to look. Don't. Cough."

Carpet sizzled under my feet, but when I reached the hardwood floor, it extinguished. Then, I became a vampire, floating in the day's recesses. I skulked in the house's armpits and its damp places, not daring to speak, drinking in bits of conversation like blood.

Their voices carried in waves and I opened my mouth, attempting to quench the fiery thirst in my throat.

"Touch... lightly... best... asleep," the man's voice said in audible fits and starts.

"Husband... gone," Mama's followed.

My mouth snapped shut, and I tasted metal on my tongue; too quick and hard on my own bite.

"I'll come... night."

"Yes... night... examine... she... quiet."

I could see that the man was dressed in a suit. A black bag sat by his feet. He held Mama's hands.

When I leaned in closer, I heard the man's voice, clear as day, "We'll figure this out."

My head relit.

I hated the man, all the men, but more than anything, I wanted to hurt Mama with every part of my being. These men were the reason Papa left, and Mama was the reason for the men.

Lust was no longer my favorite circle of hell. How could it be when I was entrapped within it? This circle, this endless loop, was the life in which Violet and I were permanently stuck. I understood the reason we were condemned to this house. Mama wanted everything, and she wanted it all to herself.

The noise awoke me from my thoughts. It was as if Violet detonated the cannon, and with it came an explosion: a blast of feathers, claws, and wheels. Then came Mama's screams; those were guttural, from a place deep within her. She hid demons, too, I'd suspected all along, and they released that day, into the air, skittering into the house's cold and moist spaces.

Had Violet heard what Mama and the man said, too—this confession they'd spoken together—right before she fell, chair and all, tumbling over and over all the way down the stairs?

23

MANY
MOONS

"Damon? Damon, where are you?" I called out in a loud whisper among the garden's trees, clutching the object to my chest. "Damon, oh, Damon! Something terrible's happened!"

"Follow the string. I'm not far."

He yanked our invisible wire, and a moonlit path opened up through the garden. He was laying in the grass behind a bench.

"My darling, what happened?" Thoughts of feathered explosions tumbled through my brain until feathers became pages and pages, books.

"What happened was..." I lost my thought. "I found something. In fact, it's not terrible at all," I smiled. "And what are you doing down there?"

He stared up at the night sky. "Admiring."

"Admiring what?"

"A thousand stars, but only one moon. It's an odd concept, really, why there can't be more moons." His fingers stroked his chin.

I nestled in beside him, my treasure close to my body, and told him, "Saturn has many moons. Jupiter, too."

"And us, with only one. Seems like someone wasn't favoring us there, doesn't it?"

For once, we agreed.

"Would you like to know what I've got here?" I asked him.

He turned to his side and caressed my cheek. "I'm always interested in what you have, dear Fiona."

"A ship's log. One of many. I've discovered piles of them in the attic."

Damon reached to take the garnet book, but I pulled away, sitting upright.

"Ah, you're awfully quick when you're strong-willed," he smiled. "It does look quite familiar."

"Let me read to you," I pleaded.

"Yes, please do."

"Close your eyes," I instructed.

"Consider them closed."

I moved to the bench. The souls gathered and trees hovered. Everyone wanted to hear, and I needed to be in a spot to adequately project to such an audience. Smiling, I cleared my throat.

"Captain's log. I have come upon the great fortune of having been bound to the sea by justice, temperance, judgment and a fool all incorporated in one ethereal feminine guise. A siren, she's not, but she wails perched atop wealth. Consider my great fortune in the discovery of this most unwitting captive land audience."

Damon smiled, eyes closed. "You read beautifully."

The words, Damon. The story, I implored him, mentally poking at our string, but he did not react.

"She needs my services, and I, her wealth. It is an even exchange in my opinion, and yet she heaves her breast to the heavens and continues to quiver in my presence."

"Mmmm. Quiver," Damon repeated and stroked my calf.

"Damon!" I pulled my leg away. "The story. Do you know what this means?"

The story, the souls whispered. *The story, the story, the story.*

Damon didn't answer.

"Damon."

He was nowhere and he was everywhere.

He was the trees and the souls and our string.

"Da - ," I was fading.

Despite my protests, the garden darkened and bushes took shapes of bookshelves, brick paths mimicked threadbare carpets, and the night flock flying overhead snored like Violet.

When I squinted to the sky, my eyes blurred, and a moon became moons became moons.

24

STUCK

"Fiona, you need to stay outside of the room while the doctor examines Violet."

"No, I need to go in."

I tried my hardest to push past, but Ms. Lally had me beat in both girth and fortitude.

"You're worried, child," she said to me, and her face twisted, contorted, like another human was hiding inside her skin and trying to come out through the space around her mouth.

Next, she did something she had never done to me. Not once, not in all the times, all the studies, the books, the lessons. Ms. Lally reached for my long braid and ran it through her fingers. It stopped me with the most meager of force, really, hardly any force at all. This act, the bizarre application of the tips of her fingers to the length of my hair rendered me temporarily speechless outside of our bedroom door. My arms exhaled into rubbery ribbons as she moved from my hair to placing her hands on either of my shoulders.

I was swept by that sensation, rocking on a drifting sea, soothed like a newborn baby whose mother has imbued it with a lullaby. She didn't groan when I placed my head on her waiting arm. Her thickness was necessary then, for it was the glue that kept me from disintegrating to pieces when my body started wracking itself with violent shivers.

Tide pools formed on my cheeks. No life sprung hence from them. I was not the ouroboros in any part. Not that day.

"Oh, Fiona. Violet's going to be okay. She took a nasty tumble down the stairs."

"But, why," was all I managed.

"We don't know why she was out of her room, but it's lucky the good doctor was here talking to Mama when she fell." Her hand moved gently to my face. "You know? We all underestimate poor Violet, but that little one's got some strength in her arms, getting all the way to the stairs like that. And you! You're never asleep during the day. Tucked into bed like you hadn't noticed anything at all." She pulled me away and placed her hand to my forehead. "We ought to have the doctor check you as well."

I shut down. A horse in a factory. A mound of nothing imbued upon itself.

The door inched open, and sounds of Mama trickled forth, intermingled with the doctor's deeper tones. His voice sounded like the man that sat with Mama earlier in the dining room, right before Violet went down the stairs and I ran to hide in bed.

Mama exited the room and shut the doctor in behind her. Violet was quiet. A sharp pinch attacked my arm and I was shuffled away, seeing the doctor for only the briefest point in time. His face and the Captain's blurred into one behind my heavy eyelids.

When I woke the next morning, all I remembered was the sound of the boots.

When I woke the next morning, all I remembered was dreaming of thick piled carpet, flooding, and feet trodding its sodden weight.

25

CROSSROADS

My retinas never fully healed back then, not after being cooked. Once I turned 18 years old, the only place I could truly see with with my damaged eyesight was in Mama's room. It was hard to say why life was clearer in there.

Dry, aching eyes are the worst kind of eyes, especially for one who makes a life from exploration, reading, writing, and absorbing information via the retinal route. But, I began to see the wicked children again, walking to and from the real school. I was taller then, and they stayed the same size they always were.

Left-right-day-night.

I never heard that song anymore, but I remembered it.

I held a large mirror at the window, aiming it at the wickedness below, but misjudged the angle and the glare reflected back upon me.

My eyes burned when it did.

Each time I went to restore myself in Mama's room, it took an unknowable amount of moons to summon the necessary bravery, and I managed it this day by way of the thick dense carpet. Trawling the attic became difficult due to the call of the

Captain's logs and those stories of wonder and intrigue on the high seas. Yes, those books multiplied over time. I could hardly move past the shiny maroon journals without stopping to read, and then time would pass in a wonky manner, and someone would eventually call my name.

This particular day's carpet walk was easy. Sundays were for Mama's dinners, so Mama and Nanny were preoccupied in the kitchen. Violet napped and the Captain was at sea. You do see it, don't you? After so many of these conversations, I've noticed that sometimes I rely on you to be my eyes when mine are, well, I feel like I've gone there enough already.

That day in Mama's room, picture cards were laid out on her cossack. They were shaped in an upside-down U, all of them down-turned except one cartoonish card. I picked it up and held it closer to my face. It showed a tall burning tower wearing an off-kilter crown, a lightning bolt crashing against brick, and two people falling to their doom. The Roman numeral 16 appeared across its bottom. A glass sat empty on the cossack, its contents red and dried around the inner bottom rim.

I didn't know how to play these cards, lacking their spades and hearts. I still don't. Despite many searches and discoveries of Mama's secret books, I never found their instructions.

When I peeked at another overturned card in Mama's U-pile, 10 swords revealed themselves.

"Aces!" I excitedly whispered, but I didn't know why I said that, and realizing something didn't feel right, glanced at the door.

Were you watching me in that room? I thought I could feel you then. I gave our string a tug, but couldn't sense you tugging back. What were you tugging in that moment, Damon?

A ship's rope, most likely.

There were so many items to find; always maximum unexplored terrain but minimum time.

Mama's second dresser drawer slid easily open despite its weight. If you must know, it's because first drawers are for undergarments. Everyone knows that, silly. But seconds, second drawers are up to the bearer. I don't know what I expected to find, but not this. I froze.

A smile played on my lips.

Good for you, Mama. You'd bested me, but only for the moment.

I pulled out the top paper in a drawer full of files. Files! In a dresser drawer! Not clothing, but papers; stacks and stacks of papers.

I spread some papers open on Mama's bed, and realized I was looking at something I'd never seen before, not in all of my books, not in everything that had been given to me since I could string together two words. The intersecting lines looked like a puzzle at first, and then slowly, my heart rate rose and I began to understand. I understood because of the view from my window and deductions from books. The train that leaves Prague. Papa's stories. But not from seeing anything like it in person. My shoulders shook, arms trembled, and fingers twitched. Oversized creased paper laid open on the mattress.

For the first time in almost two decades, I was looking at a maze of lands, rivers, lakes and oceans. Graphite X's, lines, and circles marred the papers. When I found the origin, my home, I realized that I hated this house more than ever. You see, I was but a speck on this funny flat vantage point called a map.

26

THE
AUTHOR

"Fiona, are you writing again?"

Violet croaked the words from her bed, my heart pounding at the realization that she could see me in the moonlight.

"Writing? No. Go to sleep, Vi."

"Fiona, that's not true," she weakly insisted. "You're always writing in those darn books."

I wanted to throw the book at her, but instead smiled at the thought of myself as the author of the delicious words I'd found in the attic. She had no idea of the secret trove I'd discovered. So, when her breathing slowed to a considerable crawl, I dove back into the storyline from my attic treasure.

Captain's log, day 34 at sea. Weather: sunny and warm. Ocean: glass with a top wind.

We've exhausted several islands in search of him, following all the leads we've been given, but also plotting a course against the stars. Her documents have been little help. After exhausting the Ursas, Perseus, Draco, and Casseopeia, we're guided now by the mighty Centaurus. I'm irritated with myself for the realization so late in this voyage, now our sixth, for missing the obvious, but I can't shake the feeling that we're close. It all makes so much sense now. He'd go where the stars point to the place two unexpecteds live in harmonious opposition.

My head and heart competed with my eyes for attention. Lids sank and myocardium pounded. Neurons fired and fought to recharge. When I woke the next morning, the journal was on the floor.

I'd dreamt that night of a half-human, half-beast fighting for its life to stay afloat in a calm sea, while a crow's carcass flew overhead.

27

TIDE POOLS

"Ms. Lally, what's outside of our home?" I asked after a discussion on Melville one grey afternoon, waiting until Violet was resting in bed.

"A garden, a cobblestone road, the waterway, the landing, a market, and a schoolhouse for wicked children," she told me, tidying up the books on our table, not responding to, noticing, or understanding the intent of my question.

"Ms. Lally, *Moby Dick* is a work of fiction, correct?"

"Fiona," she laughed, her ruffled white shirt heaving. "Of course, it is. Do you truly believe that there is a white whale seeking revenge on a singular sea captain?"

"Or, for that matter, that there is an entirety of a vast ocean out there, beyond the one sea where the Captain boards his ship?" I asked.

"There's a whole big world," she dropped the statement in mid-air, and I watched it pool on the floor.

Actually, we watched it together, her and I; me with intrigue and her with furrowed brows as all five words that dripped from her mouth soaked into the worn wood and disappeared.

"Fiona, what's your question?" I'd annoyed her.

"Ms. Lally, where do you go when you leave our house?" The words poured from my mouth.

She was silent.

This question pooled on the floor, but did not soak into the wood. She would have to step around the puddle when she needed to maneuver. We all would. I created a new lake on our bedroom's map, one that had not existed previously, and there it sat in the middle of the room, staring us in the face.

"The garden," she brusquely answered, staring out the window. I couldn't tell if she was thinking, didn't want me to see her expression, or was looking for the answer, but her reflection only showed a downturned smile that resembled sadness. Or fear. Perhaps both.

Anger?

"Why?"

"Well," she frowned, "to think."

"Ms. Lally, I've been thinking."

Violet attempted a laugh, but her snide caught her off guard and she hit her head backward on the headboard. Ms. Lally rushed to her side and they both shot me a nasty look.

"If Papa left, and we only have the garden, and," I got up and looked out the window, "and, there's the channel with the ships and then there's Papa's university..." the thought formed wildly in my head. It was a tangle of brush and twigs, but in that mess I saw the buried gem. I looked at Violet and saw it forming there, too—I saw it sparkling in her eyes! "We should be able to find him. He's got to be right here."

"Ms. Lally?" Violet's voice was quiet, but she was following me, and for the first time in a long time, we were in it together.

Ms. Lally fiddled with her skirt. Had we captured something in her imagination? Twirled it around on a stick and tangled it?

"Fi, put me in my chair and roll me to the window," Violet instructed.

I did as asked and rolled her to the window in a direct and smooth path. "Can you see?"

"You mean past all the smudges on the pane? Goodness, Fi."

I swirled the smudges around with my dress' hem.

"We should make a list of all the places we can see, and then, Ms. Lally, you can double check inside and around each one for Papa..." Violet's voice trailed.

"What is it?" My heart beat like a thousand bird wings trapped inside my chest.

I watched Violet's face sink, dribbling over her tiny protruding belly, and wax surreptitiously over her unusable stick legs before she said it to me: "If Papa was right here, and we could find him..."

"Yes," I vigorously nodded, "Go on."

"Then why wouldn't he simply come back to us?"

We both turned to Ms. Lally, who was sitting at the small table, head hanging forward, face drained to the color of the sky when the channel was about to burst with storm.

"Excuse me, girls, I must use the powder room. We'll continue this another time, but it's quite urgent."

When she left, she closed the door behind her.

When she closed the door behind her, she did something she almost never did, and slid the key in the lock.

When she locked the door, and I was sure Violet was content to stare out the smudges for a while longer, I quietly pulled Mama's map from my pocket and laid it across the floor.

When I was able to locate Nantucket on the map, I realized that Moby Dick was not fictitious. My retinas finally collapsed as the room grew dark in a rapidly narrowing circle, and the increasingly large pool at my feet was no longer metaphorical.

28

BANG, BANG, BANG

It's hard to talk about a cooked retina. I'm sure you understand. It's easier to talk about cooked delights, like puddings and steaks. But, I don't have stories about those. Not now, after my appetite was all but destroyed.

I've been putting off describing what I saw that day, that day way back, so long ago, when I saw Mama with the Captain. You remember me telling you about it, don't you? While I couldn't understand it, I felt it deep in my stomach like something hit me hard. Damon, you've told me about seasickness, so I imagine that's what this was. Landsickness. A rocky, woozy, off-kilteredness of a stormy hallway carpet that squished for the boots of men. I know you remember that day, because we've talked about it. It was the day I was set to go to the widow's walk, and running down the hallway, I'd looked left into Mama's room.

Damon, I've told you about Papa's stories before, right?

Mama was on the bed

-the carpet sways-
on her hands and knees
-back and forth-
he was behind her
-Papa said you hold your fingers like this-
rocking like a ship
-draw-
I couldn't see her face, but I knew
-I'd blow him away in a fury of bullets-
that he was hurting her
-back and forth-
because he hurt me, too,
-bang, bang, bang-
then collapsed on her, smiling.
-because that's how the west was won.-

29

FEVER
DREAMS

As the blindness grew, I tried to excuse myself to bed during lessons, like Violet did when days got the best of her. The blindness came from both outside and inside. My brain was leaking in on itself, bursting its own vessels, trying to remove the parts that it no longer wanted to keep. It got better and worse over the years, progressing and receding with the tides and the moons.

At first, Nanny called Ms. Lally, who wanted Mama to call the doctor, but Marlow and I declined and said it was an affliction that couldn't be fixed by modern medicine.

"Her soul's been blinded," Marlow said. Marlow couldn't always be trusted, but in this, he was correct.

"My soul's been blinded, Nanny," I explained, whimpering.

The women worked together to cool me with cloths while Violet watched on, but from that moment, I knew I'd forever been split into two: the part of me destined to the bed, forever the girl watching Mama, and part of me floating away from myself, watching the frenzy of nonsense trying to extinguish the burning in my third eye.

"No Mama!" I was telling them not to call for her, or I was warning her. "No, Mama…" Still, she came with the doctor and more cool cloths.

Winter quickly became summer in the bedroom, and then the fireplace roared from somewhere deep inside my body. I was inextinguishable. Marlow, where was he? Where was he?

"Papa! Help! I need you!"

"Violet? Violet! Help Mama! She needs help!"

Violet was crying and then Mama was crying. The light in my eyes burned bright, and I kicked at the hands on legs, but they were steel, trapping me, damming me to this house, this circle of hell in which I resided.

A man's voice promised that it wasn't going to hurt, but it did hurt, dammit, it hurt, it hurt, it hurt, it hurt every time we went through this.

"Damon? Damon?" I floated among my friends, the trees, that night. "Day-mon? Are you here?"

"Fiona, why are you walking on tiptoes, acting like a spook?"

"I've come undone, Damon."

"In which manner of the word?" He stroked my hair and pulled me in towards him, but I had to keep a modicum of distance while I explained the serious nature of this bodily separation. I knew part of me was still sleeping in the bed, forever destined to that bedroom, forever to be a child burned into Mama.

"In the West, you hold your fingers like this," I held my fingers, "draw," two, the middle and pointer right into the space between his eyes, where his third should be, and "BOOM," I proclaimed in a hushed yell, so as not to awaken the spirits.

"Rat-tat-tat-tat!" Damon shook me by my shoulders. "Like this, right?"

He laughed and laughed, and paraded around the gardens on a horse that wasn't there, hooting and hollering in a yell barely above a whisper, whipping a false lasso above his head.

I stood from a distance, watching.

As a ghost of my former self, I realized I didn't have the heart to tell him. It wasn't like that. Not at all.

He dismounted and invited me to leave the house.

It all seemed so natural, one moment weaving into the next, until we were imagining a full tapestry of this new life.

The ship was about to embark on its greatest voyage yet. He could sneak me aboard under the cover of night, but I had no time to think.

"It's not forever Fi. I'll bring you home next time we dock. Think of your chance to finally get out and see the world!"

Dreams of Nantucket danced in my brain. The channel's churn called to me in three thrashing syllables: "Fi-O-Na! Fi-O-Na!"

I turned to the great oaks, imploring their advice. They said, "Go, my dear. We'll watch over Violet. This is a once-in-a-life-time chance."

The last thought I had before I said yes to Damon was: maybe this was what Papa wanted for me all along. He was trying to lead by example.

When I reached for my neck, the octopus diamond awaited my touch.

"It's gorgeous, Fiona. I see you're all packed."

"Yes, apparently, I am."

The night sky illuminated the garden, and for the first time in ages, I could see. I could see—not only from every facet of my eyes, but from every fiber of my being. I followed Damon out of the gate, knowing he would lead the way to the docks, and the only goodbyes I left were in my thoughts.

I.

There's a quiet knock at the door before it opens.

Dr. Pedersen: Mrs. Teuling, welcome. Please come in and have a seat. Would you like a cup of tea?

I'm seated at my desk, and when the woman enters, I remove my glasses and smile. The case sounds complex and I look forward to this conversation.

Freja Teuling: Thank you, yes. Tea would be lovely.

She removes her coat and scarf and hangs them on the rack. When she sits, she barely fills half of the chair. She is mid-advanced age. Gaunt. Well-groomed. Black dress. Wears a black pendant necklace. Her hands shake. Neuroses?

Dr. Pedersen: I'm glad you came to me today. I understand this will be Fiona's fourth adult inpatient admission.

Freja Teuling: Her fifth, technically, but the last one wasn't a hospital. It was supposed to be a home retreat in the countryside for her well-being, but I'm afraid I got taken on that one.

The woman's face reddens. She sniffs and wipes at her left eye.

A knock arrives on the closed side of the office door, and Glenna appears with tea for Mrs. Teuling. Glenna departs and I take a notebook and pen from my desk and sit in my own chair next to the woman.

Dr. Pedersen: Mrs. Teuling, we do many things for the well-being of our children. It does no good to be hard on ourselves for forces out of our control.

The woman takes a sip of tea and sets it on the side table.

Dr. Pedersen: We have much to discuss. I believe it best to start with the reason you're here. Then, we'll go into the history. Tell me, why do you feel that Fiona needs continuation of her treatment, and why aren't her needs being met?

Freja Teuling: She's gotten worse since Violet passed away. I can't handle her on my own at home.

The woman fumbles with her necklace.

Dr. Pedersen: Violet is Fiona's sister?

Freja Teuling: Yes. They were twins.

Dr. Pedersen: Were they close?

Freja Teuling: Quite. They had their differences, but they were each other's lifeblood. They grew up in the same bedroom. I had them homeschooled by a prominent teacher.

Dr. Pedersen: And as young adults?

Freja Teuling: They held their place in the home. Well, Fiona as much as she was able. Violet didn't have the physical capacity.

Dr. Pedersen: Ah, yes. I saw Violet's condition in the chart. Significant physical deterioration. Rapid, from an early age.

Freja Teuling: From birth. It was as apparent as night and day when they were born. We'd been warned that it can happen with twins. The doctor called it a horrible name, a vampirism of sorts, where one twin takes the over the nutrients of the other in the womb and the smaller one is born sickly. The smaller one was my sweet Violet.

Dr. Pedersen: Yes. I'm familiar. One twin is known to dominate the fetal blood supply in utero. And Fiona, evidence of neurologic damage from birth?

Freja Teuling: I don't understand.

She picks up the tea cup and it shakes against the saucer as she takes another sip.

Dr. Pedersen: Often, when the larger, physically capable twin takes on more blood supply than it should, blood clots can arise in the smaller vessels. The physical damage is usually hidden in the larger limbs of the body, but can manifest outwardly if it causes oxygen restriction to areas of the brain. This is likely what you're seeing in Fiona; the cause of her behavior. Damage to the frontal lobe, etcetera.

A small cry escapes the woman's lips, and she places the teacup and saucer on the edge of the doctor's desk.

Dr. Pedersen: Mrs. Teuling, has anyone ever explained this to you?

Freja Teuling: No. Not like this.

Dr. Pedersen: Ah. We will take it slowly then. This will be for the good of Fiona.

She nods.

Dr. Pedersen: Violet had other physical manifestations of this syndrome?

Freja Teuling: We knew her ability to walk would deteriorate because of the muscles in her legs, and a doctor told us she couldn't have children. Not that we'd put her in that position, mind you. She ended up with blindness in her left eye over time. The sun always seemed to disagree with her. It would fatigue her very quickly. Her skin was paper-thin and couldn't hold up to bruises and scratches. It was a very, well, visible illness. The skin, the easy bruising, she was so little. Her coloring always made her look sick, so it was hard to get true sense of her good and bad days until it neared closer to the end.

Dr. Pedersen: Ah. A ghostly appearance.

Freja Teuling: No. Not particularly. More purple.

Dr. Pedersen: The result of her own micro-clots in the small vessels throughout the body. Yes, yes, that makes sense. Violet exhibited one continuous bruise, a constant breaking down and re-healing. Tell me, was she always coughing? Gasping for air?

Freja Teuling: Always. It was as if she couldn't get enough in her lungs.

Dr. Pedersen: You see, it wasn't just the lungs giving her a problem, although they were part of the issue. Her body craved oxygen, and she coughed as a result of this craving, trying to get as much air into her body as possible. These diffuse bruises meant that all her tissues were as the equivalent of a "living death," as you'd have it. The breakdown was likely to emit a certain... chemical scent that would have been specific only to her. It's something you might have noticed.

She nods. It's almost imperceptible, but it's there.

Dr. Pedersen: It says in her records that she was very bright and dedicated to her studies despite all of her medical problems. Violet's a specimen I would have appreciated examining in her living days.

The woman is silent for several minutes.

Dr. Pedersen: Mrs. Teuling, I'm sorry for your loss.

She wipes her eyes. A thin smile passes her lips.

Dr. Pedersen: I'll go through and more fully explain the physical manifestations in Violet, but only if you'd like. Mrs. Teuling, would you like that?

The woman says nothing.

Dr. Pedersen: Shall we break for today? Continue this tomorrow?

Freja Teuling: That's a good idea.

Dr. Pedersen: Excellent. I'll have my secretary arrange it.

Freja Teuling: And what of Fiona in the meantime?

Dr. Pedersen: I assure you, she's under the best care.

The woman stands to leave and Glenna appears with boxes of books the woman has brought in.

Glenna: They're some of Fiona's journals.

Dr. Pedersen: Thank you, Glenna. Please set them down.

I turn to Freja Teuling.

Dr. Pedersen: Tomorrow. We'll begin again tomorrow. And, my apologies for referring to Violet as a 'specimen.' Purely medical term, you see.

30

MANY WORLDS

I cried and cried.

Through my tears, the world was an ocean, not a channel. A large white house lodged in the attic of my thoughts, but the house and its contents were distant echos. In accepting Damon's invitation, I stepped into a space unbeknownst to me for my entire awakening.

Dehydrated, a shiver traveled my spine and I dried clammy palms along my skirt. I was no longer a girl standing in a garden. I was a girl upon an enormous clipper ship.

The ship was still and I stood on its top deck, left side, peering out over the yellow glass sea that extended into the horizon. A cotton-candy pink hue lit the sky. My hands blended with the oak wood under my tight grip.

Oak. The word struggled in my mouth and I fought for something else, another name in another time and place, but the sentiment broke apart to dust.

He coughed behind me before his splintered hands enclosed my waist.

Damon.

Braids were pushed from my neck and parted lips placed on my skin. His tongue was sandpaper. I let it roam but all it did was scratch.

"Sea Snatcher got your tongue?" He growled low and soft into my ear.

A dust cloud burst from my lips and settled overboard. When I looked far down into the water, I saw the ship's brown side reflecting a swaying green in the yellow sea.

After several attempts, words choked forth.

I turned to Damon and stammered, "Is this real? This, all this." I gestured to the pinks, yellows, and murky greens and then grabbed at the rail; something real to grasp.

"Ah, Fi, real is relative," Damon answered. His body blocked my view of the ship.

"What does that mean?"

His hands on mine, and mine gripping the ship, he said, "Position and velocity are not real, because they are immeasurable. Variable, thus relative. Are we stationary? So, it would appear. Are we on a ship in a sea? So, it would appear. Are we," he paused and traced a finger down my skirt, "attached by the invisible string of the universe?"

I felt him swallow before he continued, drawing that finger up under my skirt. "Ask yourself, Fiona, does it feel real to you?"

When I didn't respond, he hugged me tighter. When our hips met, parts of me became less like sandpaper.

"This feels real," I finally said.

Slowly, I felt his body respond to my words, like I'd incanted a summoning spell. Pushing myself deeper into him, he continued to speak.

The words were strained: "Maybe there are many Fionas in many universes all doing different things at the same time."

I mimicked the rocking movement of absent sea waves, eyes closed.

"Oh, my," he choked, gripping the rail behind me, "and maybe there's a Fiona somewhere else doing something... oh, my..."

We were sandpaper no more.

When he quieted, I looked at his face. "Fiona, look out!"

It was the last I'd heard as Damon threw me to the deck. I never saw them coming, the rocks. I wasn't paying attention as the version of Fiona in this cotton candy world went down to the ship's planks pummeled by a salty-aired, sugary bliss.

31

HAIR OF
THE DOG

"When does it stop moving?" a slurred voice asked.

My eyelids were heavy. The bed was rough and the pillow flat. Little light filtered into the damp space. A few minutes passed before I realized the voice was a disembodied version of my own, asking the question from somewhere far away.

"Ha! We haven't left the channel yet, Fi!"

Damon, I thought. *You're still here.* Eyelids continued to struggle and when he came into a blurry image, something unholy spewed from my mouth.

"That's it, dear girl, get it all out," Damon said.

Groans echoed back in my face from a wretched bucket. I wiped my lips.

Damon laughed and rubbed my hair. "Drink this." He handed me a small glass. "They call it 'hair of the dog.'"

"Smells like piss."

"I didn't say sniff it," he laughed again. "Pinch your nose and down the hatch."

Swallowing hard, I gathered my resolve and forced it down, immediately regretting the decision, but willing it not to come back up. I stood and tilted with the channel's rocking. The room was small and wood-paneled, and the walls were close enough to catch me if I tipped.

"Sea legs, Fi." He bent himself at the knees in a wide stance. "Move against the motion of the ship. Better to learn it now, rather than when things get rocky out there."

Following his lead, I noticed how quickly I got the hang of it, and how abruptly the world began to right itself after Damon's dog hair drink.

"Rocky?" The word floated through my brain, and I snapped into panic. "Damon, I don't remember what happened last night."

"That's usually what happens with the stuff, especially the amount you had."

"I don't remember having anything. I never asked for any-thing."

"That's true," he rubbed my hair.

My head dully ached and when I started to tip despite a sea-leg stance, I knew it was me swaying more than the ship. "Last night. We... we... the rocks. I hit the deck."

He leaned in, pressed my back against the ship's cabin wall and kissed me.

My back against the wall.

My back against the cabin wall.

The cabin wall.

Of a ship.

I pulled away slowly and felt along the smooth wood, gripping as hard into it as my fingers would allow.

"Are you okay?" Damon asked.

When it hit me all at once, I felt my body lose control over itself. Everything shivered, from the soles of my feet to my center of my eyeballs. Dropping to half my height, Damon caught me and the sea legs caught me. Saliva overflowed my cheeks.

"I'm out of the..."

"Yes," he smiled.

"I'm out of the..."

"Yes! Say it!" he cheered.

"I'm out of the house."

"You, my sweetness, are on The Mythical Vibration, the ocean's finest vessel."

Straightening myself, a wicked smile overtook my face. "Damon, you took me out to sea! What's our mission? Are we off to find treasure? A white whale? Gold and silver?"

"Not gold and silver, but a treasure to be sure," Damon stomped his foot and slapped his knee.

"Rubies and jewels?" I laughed.

"Well, not quite, but it's very special!" Damon smiled.

"The most precious thing in the world?" I yelled and jumped, completely unsure of what the most precious thing in the world could possibly be.

"Fiona, first things first. Would you like to see the ship?"

I let the wicked smile return to my face. "Show me the decks," I ordered.

32

THE MYTHICAL VIBRATION

"Now, tell me again the first law of the sea," Damon said after we spent hours greeting The Mythical Vibration.

The sun warmed me in a way to which I was unaccustomed. This was a mystical, tentacular sun, directly smothering my face in particulate light. The morning began with a pinch in my veins that heated me to my core. It filled me with certainty that our voyage was one of joyous hope, discovery, and undoubtedly, of riches, whatever precious items they may be.

"The first law of the sea is that," Damon's voice joined with mine as he rolled his arm around my neck, "there are no laws of the sea!" Our voices rang together into the breeze and we laughed like exhausted drunken maniacs.

Damon and I explored every inch of the decks. We spied around smooth edges of three main masts as we poked and prodded from fore, midship, to aft. Peaking over the edge of the bow, Damon pointed out the figurehead on the ship's front.

The Mythical Vibration was spearheaded by a fish-like woman with long brown hair, bound legs that resembled a fluted tail, and two massive black wings sprouting from her back.

When no one was looking, we counted jibs, foresails, mainsails, and mizzen sails. We counted peg-legged men and two-legged men, one-eyed men and two-eyed men.

Damon raised fingers as he spouted statements like, "Then, there's Huckleberry, a boatswain, he's a good one, but gotta keep him liquored up. You don't want to see Huck without the Dutch courage, but there was that time that he fought Boomer because he went cold turkey and landed in the doldrums, and, oh, well, Boomer's the gunner. You see, the gunner works the artillery, but he's also got Davey to his roster, so don't be surprised if you see Davey loading the smasher, though it's not his job. You'll get it all in time, good girl."

I doubted that very much, but I grabbed onto as many of his words as I could.

"Damon, what's your job on the ship?" I asked, despite my hesitation. He seemed young compared to the worn faces we'd passed, the sneers that leered in our direction.

"Well, I'm glad you asked. I happen to simultaneously have one of the most dangerous and most important jobs on The Mythical Vibration. I'm its first mate, assistant to the Captain himself."

"Powder monkey!" a voice yelled from a shadow. "Tell the wench the truth!"

"You're groggy, Huck!" Damon shot back at the darkness.

"Anyway, this back sail, she's called the 'spanker,'" Damon winked. "And you can remember the port side of the ship is the left side because port has the same number of letters as the word 'left.' And starboard is the right side of the ship because starboard, well, it simply is."

"Damon," I said. "where's the plank?"

He yanked me behind a large barrel and we crouched low. "Fiona. You don't want to see the plank. It's below deck and you need to pray on all of your moons that you never meet it."

A heavy bell sounded three times on the main deck. I flinched.

"Why would I worry about the plank if there are no laws of the sea?"

"There may be no laws of the sea," Damon kissed my smiling mouth, "but there are rules on the ship. If you want to be part of The Mystical Vibration's crew, the first rule you need to learn is that when the departure bell rings, it's all hands on deck. We don't tolerate loose cannons."

"Aye, aye, captain."

Damon's voice shrunk to a serious whisper. "I would be very quiet about addressing anyone as 'captain' 'round here other than the real Captain. He's a bit... particular."

"Aye, aye, seamen."

"Aren't you funny," he winked. "Follow me."

"Why is the ship named The Mythical Vibration?" I called after him as he rushed to the lineup. He was adept at navigating the ship, swinging on ropes like a monkey in trees, jumping from this barrel to beam to that post. I felt like a right-footed girl with two, possibly three, left feet stumbling after him.

"You'll get your bearings," he called back, "and you'll see once we set sail!"

Something flashed in my brain as men whizzed past, swinging towards the midship.

"Damon, wait! Tell me about the rocks! I thought we already set sail! Why is the ship moving? Who threw the..."

"What rocks, Fi?" he yelled from somewhere unseen.

"Earlier? Yesterday? I'm not exactly sure." It was hard to determine time here.

"Earlier when? What is time when there's only ever a now? Come on!"

A burly man was stuffing a rod into the center of a large cast iron tube. Damon pointed to him and mouthed, "Boomer."

The sight of the cannon triggered a nausea in my gut as my eyes darted around for a clock. My stomach was signaling my brain that I had a job to do. The blue oblong disk was at almost full height into the hazy pink sky, and instinctively I turned for... for...

Something danced in the periphery of my thoughts, but I couldn't bring it to the forefront.

"Damon! What do I do?" Sweat poured from my skin, tears leaked from my eyes, and I crouched and covered my ears.

The man lit the cannon's wick and below the black tube, I saw thick soled shoes that forced bile higher into my throat. Swallowing hard, I braced for impact. *11:34 and all's...*

...the slightest pop...

...as a flock of birds released from the cannon's mouth...

...purple-golden wings shimmering over the water as they flew...

and a gagging sound, which for a moment, I questioned if it came from my own orifice, but my mouth was a sealed line. The cannon's mouth sputtered and coughed, and out came an emetic bundle of matted and thinned black feathers clinging to an emaciated clawed creature.

"Birds?" I asked, my voice shaking.

No one answered, not Damon, Huckleberry, or even the peg-leg man that was as big as he was round. Not even the skinny pale one with the mop swabbing the deck.

The last bird-thing twisted toward the water with no fight in its body, then wobbled its wings, hovering in uneven circles. One loud bell distracted my attention and I never saw the bird's final destination.

On deck, we all fell into a line. I tried counting, but Damon pushed me back and I couldn't see to the end. There were at least twenty of us, maybe more. We waited at the ready, and then I heard it. A sound that you only need to hear once to never forget.

The boots. The awful noise they made when he trudged. He walked with the weight of water.

My heart pounded.

Thud.

Thud.

Thud.

His sound reverberated to such a degree that no one could tell—I looked to my left and right, and we all had the same confusion on in our eyes—the direction from which he entered.

When he arrived at the lineup, he stopped at every sailor. Towering over each person, he leaned down and peered into their eyes.

"Hrumph," he said, and moved on to the next.

When he stopped at me, he glared, silent. Something pinched into my wrist. I rubbed a sting that was not there. He continued to Damon.

Peered.

"Hrumph."

Continued.

To the end of the line.

The bell tolled a single ring and the line disbanded.

"What just happened?" I whispered to Damon.

"What do you mean?" he laughed.

"I mean, what was that?" I asked, my breath caught in my throat.

"The Captain gave us our orders." Damon's eyes glittered in the sunlight.

"He didn't tell me anything," I insisted.

"Lucky you! Come on, we're setting sail!"

II.

The day rises as the one before and the woman is here in a green dress. She waits for me to initiate conversation. There is no teacup in her lap, but her gaze is occupied by boxes of books stacked near the window.

Dr. Pedersen: Before we begin with the journals, let's start from the sisters' relationship. Tell me about them as children.

Freja Teuling: They were closer when they were younger, when they were more like each other.

Dr. Pedersen: Like each other in what way?

Freja Teuling: Physically. Mentally.

Dr. Pedersen: Before the illness started to reveal itself through sicknesses and puberty?

Freja Teuling: Yes. It wasn't so obvious when they were five, six, even eight years old. Well, maybe to them it wasn't as obvious because Violet could still walk. They loved story time together, especially with their father.

Dr. Pedersen: Tell me more about that.

Freja Teuling: He played a major role in their studies, leading them through lessons he considered important. My husband was a university professor and a natural storyteller. He was a special man, always on this quest to find an answer. Before he left—

Dr. Pedersen: The children's father left?

Freja Teuling: Not intentionally. It's a long story.

Dr. Pedersen: Would you like to tell me about your husband leaving?

Freja Teuling: I thought we were discussing the girls' relationship.

Dr. Pedersen: Let's revisit your husband leaving.

Freja Teuling: We'll have to. It's important.

Dr. Pedersen: I've made a note.

The woman's hands wring in her lap. It interests me how the lines on her face change with the mention of the husband. I write "abuse?" on the notepad, but watch the woman for another minute more and cross the word from my list.

33

HEAD OF A
PIN

As The Mythical Vibration set sail from the yellow glass sea and out into open waters, two things happened. Damon warned me—I'd notice it as we travelled along the channel—that the change would occur when I saw the white house shrink into the distance down to the size of a dot.

His arms wrapped around mine as I stood aft watching the house grow ever smaller. It was a strange house to view from afar.

"You'll see, it will grow so tiny it will appear like the head of a sewing pin. When we hit that point, that's when it will happen."

"What's going to happen?"

"We're going to flip along the infinity."

Standing at the ship's stern, I watched a white house with a widow's walk and stained glass windows until my vision grew tunneled. I stared until I was seeing down the shaft of a hollow-bore needle, focusing until my periphery blacked out. I watched until I was sitting in the cinema, like one described in my books, looking up backwards at the projector. The home in the distance became a mother's inverted headache scotoma. When it all came to the pinhead, I gave in and rubbed my eyes with a vigor, and in a flash of stars, it happened.

"Did you notice it? We flipped," Damon whispered. "Our adventure begins."

We entered new waters of crystal sheen, sparkling emerald greens with clarity to depths so great, to look straight down created a dizzying effect. Glass shapes floating on the surface broke when one looked up and realized it was the cotton candy pink sky eyeing its beauty in the mirror. Clouds of blue floated past in lazy rivers, shaped like auspicious animals in agreeable poses. These were tea parties in the heavens where a rhino shared a biscuit with an alligator. I drooled at the thought.

"It's like this: picture the infinity symbol, essentially a figure eight turned on its side. We sailed along one of its curves, and when we reached the midpoint, we flipped. It all flipped. It's really quite straightforward," Damon explained, still harboring my body with his.

Here in the flip, I moved free of his protection and he did not struggle against me. This was a new world. Damon smiled at me as I smiled back.

Real sun heated my skin, and I let Damon watch as I removed my dress, folding it aside for cooler days. Next, I unplaited my hair and pinned it to a high bun atop of my head. I tucked my petticoat over itself a few times at the waist, reveling in the salt breeze against my legs and the air against my bare neck. Closing my eyes, everything smelled like brine, and my mouth puckered with its newfound saltiness.

I expected a kiss in return.

Nothing.

"Damon?" I opened my eyes.

He'd disappeared. The stern was empty save for the tall scraggly man I'd seen earlier, still swabbing the deck. The mop moved back and forth for a job, it appeared, that would never be done. When he looked my way, his face turned a bright shade of magenta.

"Damon!" I broke from the mop man's gaze and shouted. "Damon!"

Damon didn't answer.

But, someone else did.

"Must feel good, the breeze on you like that." This was a new voice; small with a tin-can echo.

I swerved around, and immediately regretted the "Ha!" that escaped my lips.

"Go ahead. Let it out. Everyone has their say when it comes to me." He was a tiny human with a flash of silver hair that made my fingers itch to touch. Small pointed ears poked out from the sides of his head. He was wearing an odd dress, like a man's white formal shirt, that hung to the floor. The bottom was clean for the way it swept the ship's planking. I looked back at the mop man, but he, too, had gone.

"Who are you?" I asked.

"'Who' is better than 'what,' I suppose," the man with the silver hair responded, exhaling and shaking his small head. "I'm Little Bard, the voice that sings to keep you entertained." His lips turned down at the corners and his head hung forward from his shoulders.

"Why are you dressed like that?" Heat flushed my cheeks.

"Oh, it's a shirt, and an unfortunate one at that. No one here knows how to sew!"

"Well, Little Bard, if you bring me a mending kit, I may be able to help you with your shirt troubles." It was the least I could do. I felt terrible for laughing at his appearance, but it was unexpected.

"That would be fantastic, Fiona," the Little Bard smiled.

"How do you know my name?" The Little Bard was coming closer. He was at once a gentleman and... not.

"Everyone on board knows your name," he giggled.

He reached out and we shook hands. His fingers barely filled my palm, but I tried not to focus on their miniature size.

"Little Bard, what's your name?"

"Interesting... I'd heard you were smarter than this," he eyed me up and down.

"Smarter than what?" The conversation was downright confusing, not to mention I was talking to a man the size of small animal with wiry hair and beady eyes. All he needed was a tail.

"My name is Little Bard. We finished discussing it not a moment ago." He was getting short with me and his echoing voice grew louder.

"I see," I stopped myself from saying too much, as I was in uncharted territory. "Your name is a mouthful. Let's settle on calling you LB. How does that fit?"

"Better than this shirt," he smiled.

"Fiona?"

"Yes, LB?"

He danced as he sang:

"When you sail the world on a whale's back

to try and break ahead of the pack

don't despair when rough seas are nigh

hold to the fin and keep that chin high

you'll think it's the water smashing about

but it's only the whale, his tale, and spout."

He continued, "Got it?"

"Yes," I said, faltering. I hadn't really gotten much of anything at all.

34

SEWN
SEAMS

Wild silver hair extended up from behind a barrel.

"You know you can ask, right? Instead of being sneaky. I see you," I shouted from my room.

Damon said this cabin was mine. The cabin was on a lower deck and held two small beds, side by side, with a table in between. I'd chosen the bed closest to the door. The room was small, windowless, and smelled slightly tonic. Plain wood planking enclosed every inch of the room. Despite the space, light streamed in from the outside and illuminated my work so I could sew without fuss. An oil lamp was left on the table, off for the day, offset with a matchbook for night's darkness.

Damon used the word "yours" in reference to the room. My heart skipped. It was the most beautiful room I'd ever seen, and I was determined to learn each notch in every plank.

LB's shirt was in my lap.

"Ask what?" LB stood behind one of the water barrels. "And, I wasn't hiding," he insisted in his tiny melodic voice. "Only resting."

"Resting while sneaking glimpses of me mending your shirt?"

"Not technically mending; my shirt was in fine condition. You insisted on tailoring it for me," he wagged a tiny finger.

"Put your finger away, LB. Your shirt was sweeping the planks. I'm mending it into pants." As I sewed, I used both of my eyes but for different purposes: one to keep an eye on the needle; the other, to keep an eye on LB. Trust was a thing to be earned on the ship, Damon warned me.

"Ouch!" I cried, a drop of blood pooling at my fingertip.

"Watch your fingers, Fiona."

"Why are you staring at me?" I asked.

"They said you were beautiful," his voice lowered.

I placed the sewing down in my lap and sucked on my finger.

"Who's 'they?'"

"Those that said it. The ones on the ship." LB's register was back in his normal spritely tone.

"Damon?" I insisted.

"I heard it before I saw you, that's all."

"And?"

He laughed. Laughed!

"Well? Do you think I'm beautiful?" When I stood, the ceiling hung inches from my head.

"Well, Fiona, do you think you're beautiful?" LB asked, his voice long and drawn.

My fingers ran through the small knots in my hair. "I never cared much for looks. I care about thoughts and being smart and knowing what was in books."

"So, then what does it matter what I think?" LB asked.

"I guess it doesn't—"

He interrupted me with a sputter and paced the room. "Who decided that tall and thin is beautiful? Who decided that long brown hair is beautiful? Your eyes are blue. Congratulations? You had no control over these things. You know what I think is beautiful? You saw my shirt dragging and decided to make it into a pantsuit. That is beautiferous."

I picked up the sewing to calm myself. "Beautiferous isn't a word, LB."

"Are you the bard or am I the bard?"

I bit the thread at the knot and tossed the shirt to him. "Here. Try this on."

He slipped behind the unused bed and into his new garment.

"It appears I've made you look like a giant baby in a one-piece suit," I smiled.

"So, it appears. And, so, I adore it. Thank you, Fiona. It fits... beautifully." LB's voice took on the quieter tone again, and then we both burst into hysterical laughter.

When we stopped laughing, he followed me out of the cabin and we walked to the main deck to peer out over the sea. It was the orange time of day; late afternoon mandarin when the water came close to joining with the sun.

"LB, do you ever tire of the colors?" The water appeared to be immediately below the ship. My sweaty fingers ached to touch it, but it remained so far from where I stood. I reached anyway.

"Can you tire of something inherently within yourself?" he asked.

"What do you mean?" One hand merged with the image of the water and they shimmered together.

"Beauty is as beauty does." He shimmered as he spoke.

I waved my hand and watched the image appear and reappear. "LB, why is treasure so important to the Captain?"

"Why is anything important to anyone?" I asked LB.

"I understand the philosophy..."

"Maybe you do, maybe you don't," he interrupted.

"But, this treasure, in particular," I turned to LB. "What is it? This is a voyage for treasure, correct? Aren't all voyages for treasure?" Echos of unfamiliar perfumes clung to my memory.

"Treasure is... yes, you said it. Treasure is particular. It's not always a thing. Sometimes, it's, well, not a thing."

"LB," I said, slowly turning to the tuft of silver. "Can treasure be a person?"

"*When the Captain returns with*
the wise man in hold
the woman in black
gives him all the gold!"

"LB!" I threw my hands in the air. "The singing! I appreciate it, but I just need to know. What are we looking for? How can I help?"

His eyes turned to mine, grew big, and darkened.

"Aye, okay, calm, my girl. The Captain gets the gold if he brings back the person. Get it? Captain in search of treasure."

"Who is this person?" my eyes shimmered.

"They call him The Philosopher. And you'll find your way, Fiona, you always do."

Something hard flipped in my stomach.

LB continued, "I'm not the best one to ask. You might want to find Davey. Davey knows all about The Philosopher."

Sweat dripped down my back. I sat against the ship's wall. "Who's Davey?"

LB hopped about on one leg. "Geez, Fiona. How do you not know Davey? Can't miss him. One leg. Smells like fish. He's the day man."

III.

8:07 in the evening. I've decided to begin my examination of Fiona Teuling's journals. They are disordered and un-dated, however, they are fairly well stacked by age, according to fade, wear, and completeness. My initial assessment is that the handwriting of the earlier notebooks is the school-age cursive of a pre-pubescent teenager, although the quantity of notes in those books are few. The bulk of the work takes place in a tighter script, and a cursory overview appears to show a more disordered presentation as the books appear newer. That is, disorder increases as the subject ages.

The books are, for the most part, a similar quality. Maroon cloth-bound with white interior pages. These are children's exercise notebooks afforded to more affluent families. Opening the front cover reveals a blank interior page. Note: I find this interesting. Whereas most children are trained to document their names on this space, Fiona has left this blank. A subsequent check of all journals reveals the same.

The book in my hand appears to be from the mid-teen years, based on the tightness of the handwriting and coherence. A sample page reads:

"The Mystical Vibration shake me and I cut a yellow glass sea like a hot knife. I looked to sky, pink, a bright burning disc sun. Then, my eyes squint to a glowing then off and blue.

I felt his presence me before his hands on my face. He pushed the hair from my neck sticky and reach in rough lips. Mouth - sandpaper.

He pulled back a little. "Sea Snatcher"

Try to see. a murky green in the.

"Is this real?"

35

DANCE FOR
ME, DAVEY

"Mmmmmmmm, you taste like a piece of salted cod," Damon said as he licked the side of my neck.

We were below the main deck, leaning against an aft cabin window. The large room held a table, some books on shelves, and felt hot and airless. I turned my face away from Damon and into the cool pane.

"Is that a compliment?" I asked. "Salted cod?"

"Do you like fish?" he purred. Our sweat mingled.

"I do," I breathed in the heavy air, trying to determine if I was feeling pleasure or discomfort.

"Then you tell me if it's a compliment." He pulled away and smiled. "How old are you, Fiona?"

"What?"

Damon laughed. I swooned with his smile and then remembered the question and pulled my face from his.

"Eighteen. Maybe twenty. I don't keep track of nonsensical things like years. Why?"

"You are so naive. Beautiful and wildly intelligent, but so naive." His fingers trailed lightly over the imprint my face left on the window.

I did what any self-respecting woman would do and stomped on his foot with my boot heel.

When he stopped howling and stared at me, I asked him 'why?' Why was I so naive? Why, Damon?

He wandered to a shelf and picked up a book. Pretending to read, he answered, "When someone is kissing you, no, wait. When someone invites you on a sea voyage, they like you, Fiona. But, you never stop asking questions. It's like the subtleties fly right over you like little birds in the sky. You," he laughed and slammed the book, "you like your evidence like this." He reached for my hand and moved it to his pants. "Hard."

"Damon!" I feigned horror, and then moved in closer so he would kiss me. We kissed for a long time.

"We should stop," I whispered. "People are watching." The feeling of bodies passing in and out of the room loomed in some far distance.

"People are drooling," he replied into my mouth.

"There are more important things than kissing," I said, although my body didn't believe it.

"Like what?" he sighed.

I pulled away and walked toward the door.

"Like how about you share something for once, since you seem to know all about me. What about you, Damon?"

"I'm the same as you," he said, hand on his hip.

"How?"

"Age-wise."

"So, you're eighteen. Maybe twenty?" I asked.

He moved closer, but I stayed near the door.

"Yes. I've told you. Time is irrelevant. I've spent my life on ships and docks, docks and streets. Streets and rocks."

"What?" I asked. "Rocks?"

"I didn't say that," Damon replied.

"You did. You just said it."

"My dear Fiona. I didn't. I said docks, ships, and streets. It's literally a life of freedom, this seaward way of being."

A fleeting uncertainty tugged at me again.

He moved closer still, and picking up my hand, placed it to his chest. "Fi, we're the same, you and I. It's what makes this," he gestured to him and me, "so special."

"But, where did you come from?"

"Fiona. Darling." For once, he looked perplexed, like he needed to think before more words bubbled from his lips. "I suppose I came from my parents."

I wasn't expecting that.

He continued, "Didn't you come from your parents?"

Tears welled in my eyes. "It's hard to remember, but yes, I suppose I must have."

"Don't be so hard on yourself. Do you think anyone remembers what they were doing eighteen, maybe twenty years ago? I barely remember if I enjoyed breakfast, although if Davey made it, I bet I loved it. It's better to think up and down and left and right, oh! Circular, even, rather than forward in a straight line. You know what happens if you try to sail through life in a straight line?"

"No," I cried.

"You hit the rocks."

"What do you mean?"

"If you try to sail though life in a straight line, and rocks appear ahead, you're going to head right for them. You've got to be able to move, dodge, dash. I think you'll figure all of this out, my love."

He pulled me into his arms and let my head rest on his shoulder while I sobbed.

"Let the saltwater out," Damon said. "No good keeping the sea bottled up inside of you! It rusts away your insides."

After a good, long cry, I dried my eyes.

Damon put his hands on my shoulders, and I put mine on his. We looked into each other's eyes, and I felt the spring of life begin to tickle the soles of my feet.

"Okay," I said. "I'm okay."

"Good," Damon replied. "Out the door."

The door, heavy and ornate seemed further away than I expected. My feet struggled with the ship, tipping forwards then backwards, feeling like I'd drunk too much wine.

"Maybe I'm not okay."

Inebriation was a sensation I'd experienced on and off since the voyage began and I couldn't shake it. Damon followed as I stumbled out.

When we stepped into the narrow stairwell that led to the upper deck, air rushed to greet me and I gulped as much freshness as I could gather into my lungs.

"Damon, how well do you know Davey?" I panted.

"Pretty well, why?" He picked up a nearby telescope and peered out into the watery abyss. Every trace of malice, anger, frustration—whatever had built from the moments prior—dissipated with the oxygen.

"Could you introduce me?"

"Leaving me for another man already?" Telescope discarded, Damon was back on me, tongue in my ear, whispering, "I've got more legs."

I leaned back into him and sighed, "No." The sky was a wild shade of magenta. I had no sense of time, but the sun was about halfway raised. A cloud with pointy fox ears floated by and something bit me in the chest. "I want to ask him about The Philosopher."

Damon backed away from me with such speed, he tripped over some piled deck rigging.

"Damon! Are you all right?" I helped him up.

"Who told you about The Philosopher?" His voice was quiet, but his tone was harsh.

"LB."

"Who?"

"Little Bard."

"Who, Fiona?" Damon demanded. His eyes grew dark.

I continued to shrink, the sound of my voice growing small with truth. "The Bard! The small one with the tiny voice and the long shirt."

He grabbed me around the arm with more than enough force. "You can't play these games on the ship, Fiona. Now I'll ask you one more time. Who told you about The Philosopher?"

The sea was smooth as glass, but we'd only been out a day, two, maybe a more. As I opened my mouth, struggling to utter words that wouldn't come, a slight shift in the ship's course threw me to the ground. Everything began to vibrate—the ship, my head, my body. Damon's image swayed like heat rising from the stove. Even my eyes popped from side to side in their sockets.

"Sea legs, Fiona."

The bell rang twice.

"I'm needed on deck. We'll continue this when you learn to tell the truth."

I watched him stomp away and disappear behind the ship's clutter. His anger was sudden, and I felt a pinch in my arm. When I looked down to swat what wasn't there, I saw the finest snag in the skin, and knew what it was. It was the string pulling from my chest through my outermost veins.

"Dust yourself off, Fiona, and next time, don't let anyone tell you what to do," the tinny voice said.

Tears welled in my eyes and I wiped them on the back of a dirty hand.

"It's just the salty air. I'm not crying. Also, you literally just told me to dust myself off." I never saw LB coming, but he always seemed close by. It was as if his arrivals were timed by both the tremors and the recoveries. I was equally relieved and embarrassed he was there.

"That's common sense; you would have dusted yourself anyway." If there was annoyance in his voice, it quickly dissipated.

"Why didn't Damon know you, LB?"

"Don't worry, Fiona, not everyone knows everyone. Now, come with me, I'm going to take you to Davey. By the way, how do I look?"

The small man twirled in his newly fashioned apparel. He looked like an overgrown baby with silvery wire hair, a pouty mouth that managed an upturned smile, and a head that still hung forward. He kicked his booted heels into the air.

"Stunning," I said with a smile.

"A wonderful lie, my friend. Now, follow me."

Main aft to mast, I trailed as LB darted from shadow to shadow. I watched him without question. No, that's a lie. I watched him with many questions, but none that I asked.

I heard his whispery sing-song melody start up again:

"Fiona, Fiona, the sea has gone wavy,

the man that you seek lost a leg in the Navy,

to get him to speak you must offer him gravy,

and say to him loudly, 'dance for me, Davey.'"

"What in the world are you talking about?" The little man was somewhat cute, but I started to think he was equal parts mad.

"Okay, the Navy part is true, but don't worry about the gravy. Do you know how hard it is to rhyme 'Davey?'" he giggled.

"Goodness, LB. You're a handful."

"I'm bigger than that." He grabbed my wrist and hid me behind a barrel. "Look, there he is, by the mainsail. You know what you have to do. Go." I felt a push behind me. "Go!"

Stumbling forward, I whispered, "Are you sure?"

He waved baby fingers at me and disappeared.

Clearing my throat, I said, "Dance for me, Davey."

The man with the wooden leg did not turn around.

"Louder!" The little voice urged from behind.

"Dance for me, Davey," I all but yelled.

Davey turned. In all his girth, as round as he was tall, the wooden leg holding him like a spoke on a wheel, he turned. Beet red in the face, pockmarked skin and nostrils flared, he looked over and ahead, then down at me.

"Say it again, girl, I dare ye." His voice was like metal grinding against metal.

"Dance, uh, dance for me, Davey?" I sputtered.

"Now ye better run."

36

HARD SEES

I'd outrun Davey, but not because of his girth or leg. The man spun like a wheel, cutting a path through the ship. No, I'd outrun him simply because I'd learned to do what LB did, and Damon, too, which was to fly across the ship from barrel to barrel, shadow to shadow. Lessons abounded on this voyage, and the sooner I picked them up, the more likely my chance of thriving.

Once safely back in the tiny cabin, I threw myself into bed. More precisely, I flung myself onto an uncomfortable straw sack on top of linked ropes on a wooden frame, of which I bounced right off and landed hard on the floor.

"Sleep tight," a musical female laugh tinkled, but no face appeared.

"What is it, now?" I groaned. I needed to acquire a weapon.

"Sleep tight. I knew you. Were coming. So I tightened. Your bed ropes. Might have. Overdone it." Her laugh was sweet. Accented. Punctuated. It was unlike anything I'd heard aboard the ship. And it came from inside the cabin.

The woman swayed into the cabin's single stream of light, and a tanned wrist encircled in gold bracelets reached out to help me up. "Here. Go easy."

Her skin was the softest I'd ever felt. She lifted me from the ground as if I required no effort, jangling with each movement.

With my eyes better adjusted to the dark, I could make out her plump berry pink lips and silken, wavy chocolate hair that fell to her waist. Two brown eyes were exquisitely placed atop cheekbones carved precisely for her face. She smiled with straight teeth and an ease that immediately told me we'd be friends. I was tall and the top of my head stopped at her neck.

"Dust yourself," she smiled, "off."

"Who are you?"

"Mykke. And you are. Fiona."

"Mykke. Are you my cabin mate?" Mykke was the only other woman I'd found on the ship, and she certainly didn't seem to belong to this group of men.

"Yes," she answered.

Mykke moved like a spirit with feet barely touching the floor. Her fingers shifted my hair from my neck and kneaded into my shoulders with force proportional to the tension that had built. I melted as her bracelets sang me into oblivion.

"Sit. Have you. Even slept?" her voice rocked with the waves.

"I have no idea how long I've been on this ship. When did we leave port?"

"Two days past. Have. You eaten? Drank?"

"I can't remember." My eyelids fought to stay open. She lifted my feet onto the bed and removed my boots.

"LB... he tricked me. He told me... Davey... I said the wrong thing. I thought I could trust LB."

"Aahhh. A lesson you. Had to learn. No doubt. Trust no one. On the ship. Fiona. Not even yourself."

"Not even..."

"Hush, hush," she sang.

"Mykke, do you know about the Philosopher?"

"Hush, hush," she sang.

"Where," I fought but was losing the battle. She tucked me under a blanket and kissed my forehead.

"To Skult Island. Three days travel. Oh. You will. Love Skult."

"Skult? I've never seen that on my maps." Fuzz, fluff, cotton—it all clogged my brain.

"Oh, it's not. On any map. Have you. Read the story? About the big. White whale. The most gorgeous places. Never are."

"Who are you, Mykke?" I pushed.

"Hush. Hush. It is better I. Don't say. You might not. Wish to. Know yet." Mykke hummed a low melody, not offering any more words.

The day covered me in darkness, and into darkness I went, sleeping a long, hard sleep.

IV.

It's discomforting to inquire with Freja Teuling the following afternoon, as the journals' presence are a distraction. Her body tenses, and the deep lines around her eyes and mouth become more pronounced each time she glances at the books. I will tell Glenna to remove them.

Dr. Pedersen: Mrs. Teuling, I'd like to begin with a journal passage. It might seem like an odd entry into conversation but it happened to be what I picked up. I'm curious if you can identify what was happening in Fiona's life when she wrote this.

Freja Teuling: I hated these books of hers. So many of them are nothing but blame that I could never explain away. These are painful, Dr. Pedersen. Each time I found one, I'd hide it in the attic. Better for all of us that way. You should have seen the stacks of them.

Dr. Pedersen: I understand. Have you read them all?

Freja Teuling: No, not all of them.

Dr. Pedersen: Do you wish to wait on the journals and discuss something else?

Freja Teuling: No... no. Hand me the one you have.

Freja Teuling takes the book and reads. Her lips move over the words as I watch her face. I watch her furrowed brows, her tensing hands. The woman looks at me.

Freja Teuling: 'It makes me dizzy. A second entrance is plucked from my memory. And what of the other side of the house? It's not hidden! Forbidden and off limits!' I don't know what this means.

Dr. Pedersen: I don't know either, which is why I was hoping you could explain. I'll do my best with interpretation. Mrs. Teuling, are there any hallways or passageways in your home to which Fiona wouldn't have had access?

Freja Teuling: When the girls were little, their father had a passageway built between our bedroom and theirs so we could check on them at night without interrupting them.

Dr. Pedersen: So the statements are true?

Freja Teuling: Well, I'd assume that depends to what you are referring.

Dr. Pedersen: Yes. Okay, so we'll start by saying that the two bedrooms connected—

Freja Teuling: In both the hallways and through the attic.

Dr. Pedersen: —yes, in both places. Let me ask you, Mrs. Teuling. Did you ever tell the girls of this attic passageway? Show them?

Freja Teuling: Heavens, no. In fact, the entrance was sealed over...

Her hand strikes her breast as her voice trails off.

Dr. Pedersen: So Fiona couldn't have known, at least not because you showed her.

Freja Teuling: I've never shown her. She couldn't have possibly known. But her words... I don't understand how.

Dr. Pedersen: Let me show you.

I hand her the passage from the journal. She reads aloud:

Freja Teuling: "...used force and my energy and I ripped the panel clean off the wall, fell backwards and made a whole bunch of noise. I yelled, 'I'm fine,' and Miss Fatty yelled back, 'no one cares!'"

She flips a page, looks at the next, then turns back. Tears escape her eyes.

Dr. Pedersen: How do you feel about Fiona finding this entryway?

Freja Teuling: Belinda Lally punished the children by putting them in the closet? I feel terrible that the children were punished in that way. In the closet, I mean. And Fiona. She wasn't a bad child. She was sick.

She avoids the question.

Dr. Pedersen: Yes, well, that's clear.

Freja Teuling: Doctor... is there more? From the passageway?

The woman's lips curl in pain. Regardless of one's position, it's never fortunate to be the bearer of difficult news.

Dr. Pedersen: Mrs. Teuling, were there other men in the home?

Freja Teuling: She knew. Oh heavens, she knew.

The woman cries.

Freja Teuling: It's not what you think.

Dr. Pedersen: I've made no judgments. I'm simply attempting to interpret Fiona's writings.

Freja Teuling: Doctor Pedersen, is there a way to un-know that which you've already learned?

Dr. Pedersen: Are you asking me seriously? Because if you are speaking of Fiona, we might discuss the possibility of electro-shock therapy or something similar.

Freja Teuling: [*sighs*] No. I mean, yes, but I wish it were true for me.

Dr. Pedersen: I understand that this is a lot to take in. While I am learning about Fiona, you are also learning about Fiona.

No one speaks for a moment.

Freja Teuling: I'm ready to know what she saw from the attic passage.

Dr. Pedersen: All right, Mrs. Teuling. Well, about that. It's more than the attic passage, actually. Fiona entered your bedroom on a number of occasions, and I think we need to talk about what she found.

Freja Teuling: I don't know that I'm ready for that.

Her hands are shaking. The woman's face is blanched. I sense some shame.

Dr. Pedersen: Mrs. Teuling.

Freja Teuling: I don't feel well.

Dr. Pedersen: Mrs. Teuling?

Her body slumps in the chair.

Dr. Pedersen: Glenna! Glenna, please come quickly!

It takes us no more than a few minutes to get Freja Teuling back to a seated position and appearing less ghastly. Glenna helps her sip some sugary tea and the woman wakes. I check her vitals and they are stable.

Dr. Pedersen: Thank you, Glenna. We'll call you if we need you again.

Freja Teuling: I feel quite stupid, Doctor.

Dr. Pedersen: Not at all. It happens from time to time. When did you last eat?

Freja Teuling: It's not my appetite. It was our conversation. I have a great deal to explain about what Fiona could have seen in my bedroom, but I guarantee there's more to it than can be gleaned from a child's journals.

Dr. Pedersen: I'm listening without judgment, Mrs. Teuling, ready when you are. Please, take your time and tell me when you are ready.

Freja Teuling: Doctor Pedersen, I'm not... I'm not, you see... I'm not...

I sit and wait for her. Her lips move but no sound escapes.

Freja Teuling: I've only ever tried to protect the children, and I know I've failed at times. But, I'm not... a whore.

The last portion of her sentence is barely a whisper. I shift in my chair and feel an urge to clear my throat. It is an instinct, one that I can usually fight, but I cough. Subtle though it is, she hears. Our eyes meet. She sits straighter and begins.

37

BUT HER
NUT

"Well, hello there, you gorgeous specimen!"

He flung his arms around my waist from behind, surprising me with such force that I tipped forward. My eyes were adjusting to the bright morning, and my stomach still settling the tiny plate of food scraps that had been left by the bed. I was only a few steps onto the main deck when Damon practically sent me overboard.

It was all bright blue that morning. The water was blue; the sky blue; and Damon's eyes reflected all the blazing blue.

"Caught you, Fi! Still needing those sea legs and we're not even moving!" he jested.

"But you knocked me..." Damon was no longer listening and pushing me starboard.

We'd arrived and anchored while I slept.

'Three days,' I vaguely recalled, three days before we arrived at Skult Island, but land appeared immediately ahead of us.

"Damon, how long was I asleep?"

Before he could answer, another sound drifted lazily into my ears. It was the tinny whistle of a little man dancing a jig down the board onto actual, earthly sand.

"The island, the island,

on no map you'll find

a boy so interested

in a girl's round behind."

"LB!" I shouted.

"Pardon?" Damon asked as he kissed my neck.

"LB," I pointed, but all that was left of the tiny feet were indents in the sand.

"PQRST," Damon laughed. "Silly girl."

"Damon," I pulled away and turned to face him. "Are we here? Skult Island?"

"Isn't she glorious?" He smiled and waved his arms to the island as if it were his own creation.

A warm sun framed a the image ahead. Tall trees with bushy green tops stood at attention inland from the sandy beach; naked-bark sentinels watching over the sea in tight, neat rows. Beyond the tall bushy-haired trees was thicket, and beyond that, I couldn't see. It all got too dense.

"Fi, look. The cliffs. What a sight!" Damon pointed to the right.

In the distance stood deep red rock formations at least three or four Mythical Vibrations tall. The cliffs were sheer, growing out of the sea itself, dotted with small holes so they resembled maroon beehives. I followed a cliff edge as far as I could see until it wrapped around the island and disappeared into the distance. My eyes were growing wavy and the mirage began to shimmer.

"Do you think that's where The Philos..." A shadow crept across his face at my near-mention. "Damon, why are we here, visiting Skult? Is this where the Philo... I mean, um, the treasure is?"

"Fi! Enjoy the fresh water! The exploration! And the best part of all—a visit with the Burula Tribe. We were invited to dinner."

"But, what about the treasure, Damon?"

"The treasure," he turned and eyed me, "is not your concern."

Something swelled in my chest as the sun beat down on my face, neck, and arms, and warmed me from the inside out. Boots into sand created a new sensation; where the boat had rocked for days, the ground now stood firmly in place. I swayed.

"Whoa, there! Haha! You'll get your land legs again. Takes a minute, but not more."

Once he uprighted me, Damon ran ahead, calling me to follow. With molasses legs through sand, I struggled to keep up.

Trying to scream his name, my mouth moved as thickly as my feet, and the words came out distorted. "Daaaaammmmoooon," the demon inside of me yelled. I didn't recognize the depth of my voice.

"Oh, my," LB's voice twinkled from behind a tree. He popped out with a round hairy fruit and handed me a half. "Drink this."

"Aaaaaa ccooooocccoooooonnnnnuuuuuutt?????""

"Somewhat. Gosh, please stop talking. It's painful to hear. Just drink."

The sip was sweet and nutty. It washed down whatever the island air had done to my throat.

"Ttttthhhhaaaat's soooo muuuch better," I coughed as my voice readjusted. "WHAT was that?"

"The adjustment. The island. The air. The sand. Who knows? The butternut helps."

"Butternut? That looks like a coconut."

"But. Her. Nut. It's a butternut."

"Got it."

"Don't think you do! Ta ta, Fiona!" He ducked and disappeared into the trees.

Preparing to trudge again, I found my feet moved freely and lightly through the sand. Ahead was Damon with a group of sailors. Huck, Boomer, Gunner, goodness, it was hard to remember their names when they all resembled grizzly men of various sizes.

Davey caught my eye and snarled. Back, I jumped.

"Down, boy," Damon ordered. "Hello, Fi. We were creating a plan of escape for after dinner."

"Why escape? I thought these people were friendly?"

"Well, they're friendly unless..."

"Unless what?"

"Unless..." Damon tilted his head and winked.

"Damon! What are you implying? You said we were invited to a dinner. Why would we dine with an unfriendly tribe?" I followed behind him through the trees and down the sandy path, pushing palmed branches from my face.

"I never said they were unfriendly. We will be dining with the Burula Tribe. The food will be fantastic, but the reception will be... interesting."

"Interesting, how?"

"Hrumph," the Captain's voice cut through our conversation.

"Yes, sir," Damon stopped and turned to me, causing me to crash into him. "He wants you silenced."

"Hrumph."

"He wants you to go pick some butternut for the gift offering. Ten should do." The men walked around us, pushing the heavy brush aside.

"Where will I find butternut?"

Damon patted me on the bottom and kissed my forehead. "You are funny. On the butternut trees, of course."

38

BREATHE A
SOFT
BREATH

I hiked back to the beach where we'd anchored in search of butternut trees. Scanning my brain produced no discernible scientific name. Scanning the beach produced no discernible butternut trees. When my neck ached from the tension of this hide and seek game, I stretched it backwards to discover bunches of fruits hanging some twenty feet overhead. The tall sentinels were butternut trees, hiding precious fruits in their hairy tops.

The problem was obvious: how to get the butternuts down. When my checklist passed shaking, kicking, attempted climbing, throwing sticks and branches, searching the ground, and concluded with a sweaty me slumping to the sand in near-defeat, my ever-present tiny friend appeared.

"I figured you'd wait until I tried it all," I said.

"Is that the attitude you give to everyone offering you help?"

"You're nice, then you're not nice, then you're nice again. I don't understand, LB."

"Right now, your job is butternut fruit, not psychoanalyzing me. Have you tried whispering to it? Gently coaxing it down?" He smiled and flourished his hand at the high fruit.

"What?" I laughed at that. I laughed at the ridiculousness of the statement, of the little man in the baby suit standing in front of me with his animal Einstein hair. "You're kidding me."

"Do you enjoy being kicked, poked, prodded, climbed, and thrown at to give up your goods?"

He got me there. "I don't."

"Breathe a soft breath, Fiona."

"What?"

"I believe that's your favorite question: 'what?' Focus. Think before you respond. It will get your father, I mean, get you farther on this journey. Ask the question in a soft breath. Speak like you want to be spoken to."

He pointed to the butternuts.

I looked up, squinting in the rays that tendriled through the trees. The world narrowed in on me for a moment in blackness, like seeing a house narrow on a horizon, and then my eyes adjusted.

I said, "If ten of you wouldn't mind joining me, I'd be most appreciative."

The trees oscillated, but it might have been my eyeballs rapidly moving back and forth. A word tried to enter my brain, but my eyelashes swept it away.

"Ny-stag-mus," LB whispered.

"What?"

"Ooooh! Your favorite word again!"

"Nystagmus?"

"No. 'What.' That's your favorite word," LB gestured.

"What?"

"Geez, Fiona. Pay attention. Look - "

High above the trees, a scrawny bird zig-zagged overhead making an awful screeching cry.

"I know, that poor bird," I said.

"No, Fiona, not the bird, look at the trees!" LB danced.

One by one, the large hairy butternuts wiggled from their branches and tumbled to the ground with as much grace and elegance as I'd ever seen in a fruit.

"Ten sweet butternuts, all for you Fiona!" he clapped.

"That's... incredible," I breathed. "But, how am I going to get them all back to Damon in time?" I could carry three, maybe four at most. LB could carry one, although I doubted that he would help.

"Have you asked them?"

"To do what?" My mood pendulumed.

"To line up and dance! Sing to them, Fiona!"

I would have opened my mouth in protest, but I'd seen too many unusual things.

Beginning with the first song that came to mind, I sang, "*When the home is good as gold...*"

LB was rolling on the ground, laughing. The butternuts stayed put.

"You liar!" I yelled.

He scrambled into the trees, his baby laugh trailing behind.

39

GLISTEN GETS IN THE EYES

When the last butternut was presented at the sailors' feet, I wiped my forehead on my shoulder.

"Don't do that," Damon whispered. "Leave the glisten."

"The sweat, you mean?"

"No, sweat comes with labor. You are glistening." He leaned close to my ear and I could feel his warm breath on my neck. His words traveled down my spine when he said, "Glisten suits you."

I forgot about hard butternut labor and the anger that swelled when he dismissed my effort. A different feeling took hold of my body; one I hadn't recalled for some time. Or had I? Time felt irrelevant.

"Hrumph," the voice rang out.

The swelling wave within me crashed and disappeared out to sea.

Ten men each picked up a butternut and formed a single-file line that extended into the trees and thicket. I looked around for Mykke, but she was nowhere. In the light of day, I wondered if Mykke had been a dream; a dehydration depiction; a starvation scene.

The sun was half-mast in the sky, and I tried to discern how much time it had taken for me to collect and carry my goods.

We walked on and on, but the sun appeared not to change its position. The dense brush again opened to sand, the horizon endless upon us, wavering like clear lines in the distance.

Damon whistled ahead, lacking in glisten. Somewhere near the end of the men, I trudged, losing salt through every pore. We followed footsteps to the left and the right of the line that Davey cut through the sand. Once in a while, a silvery glint flashed in my periphery and a lyrical note carried on the breeze.

"How much longer?" I whispered when I was sure I'd seen him.

"It's straight ahead," he said. "Use those beautiful eyes."

When thirst addled me and I'd become delirious inhaling sand, a castle oasis rose before us. It dripped of coral in meandering towers, glistened with oyster shell shingles, and never seemed to stay in one place. The heat of the island created the illusion that it was moving. Or, so I assumed.

A group of something both like and unlike humans stepped out of the main gate. They walked across a drawbridge spanning what may have been water, but oozed with a cloudy thickness.

There were nine of them, four men and five women, each more beautiful than the next. The last woman was the smallest. I guessed her to be around seven or eight feet tall. They had tanned skin that mirrored the dense sand upon which they stood, and both men and women wore dark hair to the waist. It flowed with the buoyancy of the sea, never a strand out of place. Each had two legs, like ribbons gliding across the ground, and two flowing ribboned arms reaching out in welcome, and then two more arms, and another two. Their bodies were strong and muscular, adorned in fine silks, robes, and jewels. The air was perfumed and delicious.

My stomach grumbled.

"Is that them? The Burula Tribe?" I tried to whisper. I couldn't break my gaze to look at Damon. It was like seeing a diamond for the first time and trying to assess the brilliance of every aspect as someone turned it in the sun. They swayed as they glided toward us, walking past the Captain and then greeting the men.

"They are the Equagga Tribe. Where'd you get a name like Burula?" Damon asked.

"From you. You said they were called-"

"-the Equagga Tribe. And there they are. Amazingly gorgeous specimens, aren't they, Fi? Come on, walk faster and say 'hello.' They make the best plum pudding."

40

BEGIN AT
THE END

Without delay or proper introductions, we filed into to the dining room and were seated.

Dinner began immediately and that was okay with me, because I couldn't remember the last time I'd eaten a real, decent meal. About thirty of us sat around a large coral table. We watched each other, politely smiling.

"Damon," I said, my knee tapping his. "What are we waiting for?"

"The Mother," he mouthed back.

Mother. A tingling cold crept into my hands and feet and the room tunneled.

Breathe, I thought as numbness and darkness threatened to overtake my consciousness.

I sat up straight and put my hands in my lap. "Which one's the father?" The words came from someone outside myself.

"There is no father," Damon said, his attention turned to Huckleberry.

There is no father.

There is no father.

There is no...

A shimmering veil descended upon the room and my ears muted all conversation. The next thing I remembered was waking with a spoon in my mouth.

"Bid I hab a seeber?"

"Sssshhhh," a tentacled arm ribboned its way over my forehead while another deftly removed the spoon from my mouth. A third, fourth, and fifth maneuvered me closer to the silky body.

"Did I have a seizure? Who are you?" My voice shook. I didn't recognize the room, with only the ornate white stalactite ceiling staring back at me.

"They call me The Mother, my brave little sweetheart." Her words burrowed into my ear like silkworms, burying themselves into my brain.

I was nestled in The Mother's arms. "Mother, what happened?"

"You fell unaware. It's like a failing of the consciousness. It happens during a time when the brain becomes overwhelmed with surprise, bodily need, emotion. I suspect we did not catch your hunger in time."

My stomach emitted a low growl.

"Yes," The Mother laughed and the gentle silkworm nestled in deeper. "That seems to be it."

She lifted me back into my seat and I realized I never left the main hall; I hadn't recognized it from a horizontal position.

"Drink this mead," The Mother said. "It will ready your stomach for the meal."

After a few sips, my shaking calmed and dinner began.

We were fed a smorgasbord that defied logic. There was Gorgan stew, a local fish delicacy; harried pie, a soft-shelled crab encased in a flaky crust; and sides like butternut mash with crumbled scallop topping. The fermented lake berry mead put the crew of the Mythical Vibration in the jolliest of moods, and I saw the Captain—the Captain!—raise his glass with a smile.

Music played from a cave-sized instrument that resembled an organ. Its large sound filled the room with an otherworldly tune both hollow and light, like an ancient tree log floating on a salty river.

"Full yet?" Damon asked after we'd all eaten our share.

"I'm full to the brim," I responded.

"Wait for this," he smiled.

Most of the anxiety that began the meal had gone, replaced by a bubbly contentedness.

A seemingly invisible set of hands passed the next course from an entryway, which was hard to understand from my vantage until I realized that the ribboned arms were long enough to form a makeshift conveyer belt. It must have come from the kitchen, its server never entering the room. A large platter was handed to one of the women, then passed to a man, then to The Mother, where it burst into flames.

She stood over the dish and waved all her arms over it, the breeze extinguishing the flames until the dish had a slight char.

"Who," she began, "is ready for the plum pudding?"

Everyone picked up a spoon and in unison, tapped the table three times.

"WHO," she said louder, "is ready for the plum pudding?"

Three more loud taps.

"Excellent," the silkworm burrowed. "We'll see who wins tonight's prize."

"A prize?" I asked.

"The person to find the plum pit is the dinner winner," Damon explained.

I giggled.

"It's no laughing matter, Fi. Moreover, if you find it, don't say a word. Hide it under your plate until dessert is finished. It's the safest way."

"Safest for what?"

The last bowl was set, and The Mother tapped her spoon three times before Damon could answer.

The organ stopped playing when The Mother's mouth opened larger than I'd seen it open all night.

What's the opposite of hollow and light?

Full and heavy.

That's the sound her voice made when she shouted, "BE-GIN!"

41

PITS A PLENTY

The opposite of ribbony, flowing arms were eyes that darted around the room as everyone lifted spoons to their mouths. Sailors ate in hesitation with slow, careful bites. The Equagga ate wide and fast. No one showed signs of having discovered the plum pit in their dessert, at least, none that were obvious.

Bite after bite, I strained to finish. It was rich and decadent, semi-sweet and velvety, the kind of temptation that in any other circumstance I'd long for. After three days of relative starvation followed by gorging, I was hard-pressed to find room in my shrunken stomach for sweets.

Damon slowly shoveled mouthfuls, chewing with care. His eyes refused to meet mine no matter how long I stared at him. I followed his line of sight to Davey. Big red Davey was ruminating, taking continuous scoops from his bowl despite it being empty. When it dawned on me what Damon was seeing, I averted my eyes. Turning away, I bumped my plate and rattled the silverware.

The slight commotion caused eyes on me, then Damon. One of the elder tribesmen must have been more astute than beautiful, because he was the one that eyed Damon long enough to turn to Davey.

I noticed first, because I turned to Damon and said, "The old one knows that Davey has the pit."

"Oh, how wicked!" Damon whispered, a small smile on his lips.

Something lit in my brain. I stood, knocking my chair backwards. "Davey!" I shouted. "Run!"

Davey's wheel fired up and within seconds, the crew was on its feet racing after Davey's single line to the door. Pits were flying from behind us, those ribbon arms pelting us like whips, those pits hitting us like rocks.

The Captain ran last. I later asked LB if it was purposeful; the Captain behind us all to protect his ship's men.

"Not this Captain, ho ho, no, not him. You'd be last in line, too, if you kept all that weight in your boots."

42

TO LOOK
AT, TO BE
REFLECTED

"Fiona! The octopus diamond! Throw it to them!"

I heard Damon's voice behind me, but I didn't know what to do with the words. Reaching for my neck, all I felt was slippery, sweaty skin. "I don't have it!" I yelled back.

We were running hard.

They were chasing us, an outright stampede, and stopping or not meant or death or life. Equine hooves like heartbeats pounded in my chest, my head, my chest: ba-da-bump, ba-da-bump, ba-da-bump, normal sinus rhythm set to an arpeggio.

"You do," his voice found my ear through the dust. "Remember how you safeguarded it. Remember..." it trailed, and I couldn't stop to turn to see if he'd fallen underfoot. I reached into my pocket, running and grasping. My hand closed around something, but when I pulled it out, a sharpened graphite pencil revealed itself. I didn't remember placing it there, but I shoved it back.

Ahead, the sea was blurred by a melting sun at its horizon, and my brain triggered a word:

mirage.

Stumbling for a few strides and regaining footing, I realized what I had tripped over. I'd knocked into The Captain, the man attempting to pass us all, but when our legs bumped, our eyes locked, and something reflected - *se mirer* - for a fraction of a second. I wouldn't have believed it if I hadn't seen it myself in the Captain's pupils.

Pure panic rose into my throat and blocked every trace of air that attempted to reach my lungs. Each step was harder than the next, until the arpeggios grew more rapid and chaotic around me.

I was slowing and they were gaining.

Ba-da-bump. Ba-da-bump. Ba-da-bump, ba-da-bump, ba-da-bump, bada-bump, bada-bump, badabump, badabump, badabump.

A voice consumed the oxygen that I fought for, and I couldn't process if the sound was behind me, in front of me, or overhead. "Remember how you safeguarded it! Throw them the octopus diamond! It's all they want!"

Sand stuffed my mouth when I fell, and my head hit hard, bouncing like a child's rubber ball. Woozy, I lifted my face for long enough to see the hazy sun at almost full melt into the sea.

Mirare.

I saw, buried deep in the recesses of my brain, the diamond's location. After coughing as hard as my diaphragm would muster and clearing the sand from my mouth, the blackened pit emerged from my stomach and flew spit-addled into my hand.

Air made a whooshing sound as it rushed into my lungs and I sucked it all in.

Turning the rock over in my hand, I realized it wasn't the diamond at all. Pitted and mucous-covered, I'd coughed up my anxiety.

"Well done, my love! You kept it hidden like a champion!"

Damon? His voice was an echo, and I tried to look for him, but my eyelids were too heavy. Sand kicked up all around. The Captain's broken-winged bird hovered in my periphery, choking on dust.

Cough, cough.

It's not the diamond, I wanted to shout. *Mirare!*

They were coming for me. A stampede of stripes, and I heard them as equine. The Captain's eyes were clear. Hoofbeats are not always horses.

"Now, throw it as hard as you can! Ready, set... NOW!"

I pitched my arm and released the blackness from my hands, coughing as it flew.

"Wonderful, Fi! Spot on!"

The arpeggios detoured and slowed, my face hit the sand, and I closed my eyes, feeling the ocean's cool water on my arms and cheeks. For the first time in as long as I could remember, I gave into the exhaustion, and trusted that Mykke, Damon, or LB would find me before the ocean swept me away.

V.

It's evening and I'm reviewing the day's notes.

F. Teuling's husband left the home in search of a cure for his ill children. His university contacts convinced him that if the medicine he desired existed, it existed in the pioneering frontiers of America. He should sail there to find the breakthrough they needed and bring it back home.

F. Teuling begged her husband not to go, but with the household help and the promise of the children being able to leave the house, he viewed this path as his only option.

He vowed to return in one year's time, but after two years, and what had been a total of 18 months of all ceased communication, F. Teuling began bargaining with local sailors to search various ports for her husband.

F. Teuling offered to pay for the sailors' services, but was swindled into payment in both coin and physicality. Therefore, the earlier days of searching for her husband led to a greater number of men in the house against her desire. She awaited their return, always to unfortunate news that they had not discovered any signs of Mr. Teuling.

The longest affair was with one Captain Nohr Rasmussen. Rasmussen repeatedly searched and returned, using F. Teuling's home for room and board. He became somewhat of a permanent fixture in the household for several years, having been deemed the most reliable of the sailors.

No word of Mr. Teuling ever emerged. Rasmussen was eventually disbanded from his service after being found having an affair with the children's nanny.

The conversation with F. Teuling was difficult.

NB (1): Post-traumatic stress disorder. F. Teuling insists that the physical relationship had not been her choice, and that the conditions not mutually agreeable. Fiona's journals indicate otherwise.

NB (2): There were others, I feared, that contributed to various forms of abuse in the household. As these are hunches and this a delicate and unique case, I'll simply document that as a general statement for now.

Dr. Pedersen: Mrs. Teuling, welcome. Please make yourself comfortable.

Freja Teuling: Thank you. I'm tired. I didn't sleep last evening.

Dr. Pedersen: That's common after a discussion like yesterday's. We will try to go easier today.

43

THOSE
PLACES
NEVER ARE

I awoke in my bed.

Voices trailed in and out of the cabin, and I pieced together that we'd made it back to the ship bruised and battered, but full and resupplied with butternuts and clean drinking water. Exhaustion was overwhelming after our time on Skult Island. The island had not existed on any map, which meant that although I couldn't locate it again, I was sure they could find me. I'd left a piece of myself behind.

Mykke entered the bunk. In the evening light, her hair sparkled. Her long arms moved with flowing grace unafforded to most women. But, it was her footsteps that made her approach obvious. She carried a dignified step that sounded heavier than others. It was a step that announced: "I am here."

"Mykke?"

Her answer held the warmth of cocoa. "Yes, my. Dear?"

"Why weren't you at dinner?"

"Darling. I am a. Bit of an. Anomaly. Best that I. Stay out. Of. The way."

"I doubt that's true."

When she smiled, her teeth lit the cabin. I wanted to touch them.

"Why would the Equagga tell us that dessert is a game and then punish Davey for winning?"

"The Equagga are never. Supposed to. Lose. You see. Insult is an. Embarrassment to. Their heritage."

"If they control the game, how did they lose? They could have simply counted plates."

"Oh, I am. Sure. They did. Count. Plates."

"Then what do you think happened?" It was hard to talk to Mykke without trying to mirror her disjointed speech and low voice.

"I know. Exactly what. Happened." She smiled again with that same glow.

"Tell me, Mykke."

"They weren't expecting. An extra. Guest. For dinner. It threw off. Their plate. Count."

"Who was the unexpected extra? At dinner?"

"My dear. It was. You."

Mykke pulled the blanket up under my chin, but it didn't stop the cold that took hold of my insides.

Me. I'd insulted an entire tribe with my unannounced presence, and then again when they tried to claim some diamond that Damon insisted I held within me.

Tears fell from the sides of both my eyes and wet the pillow.

"Don't cry. It is all. Over." Her long arm stroked my hair. "You are. Safe."

"Mykke, can the Equaaga swim?" my voice trembled.

"Oh, yes. They practically merge. With the water. It is like. An effortless dance. Quite beautiful. To see." Her rocking voice attempted to counteract my shaking, but the shaking only intensified. "Sweet girl. You gave. Them your. Beautiful diamond gift. It is all. Over."

Ocean roiled in my gut, and I didn't have the heart to tell this woman that I wasn't safe. We weren't safe. I'd added insult to insult, and what I'd thrown at the Equagga wasn't a diamond at all, but the darkest part of myself covered in spit.

44

SCRAP RAT

The night's journey was one of fits and starts; fits of waves and rocking, starts of dreams and nightmares, each interrupting and intertwining with the other. I awoke on the floor, bed disheveled, hair amiss, clothes entangled. Mykke was already gone and her bed was made, neat with tight corners.

"You know how to use a bed, I presume?"

I jumped, unaware that LB was in the doorway.

"LB, goodness, you startled me."

"I normally don't spend much time in here, but watching you sleep is highly entertaining. You don't stop moving!"

"The ship was tortuous last night. So rocky." I stood up and tried to smooth out all the wrongs about myself.

"The ship sailed smooth as silk last night, sweetheart. I think the rocking was you, hoo hoo!" He slapped a small hand on a small knee.

"What time is it?" I rubbed my eyes.

"Time for you to find some breakfast, my dear! You're well past due for talking to Davey about the Philosopher, too. I'd say, put it on your day...

It's never a bad way
to start your seaside day
by saying, 'Davey, hey,
what's the Philosopher's way?'"

"Yes, geez, thanks," I mumbled, heading for the door. "I needed a song this early in the morning."

"Why shouldn't I sing today? We're off to Oceanus Mundi!"

"What's Oceanus Mundi?"

"*Whats ocean mumble mumble*? You're not a morning person, are you?" He picked at his pointy fingernails.

"LB, I feel as though I've barely slept. Please just tell me where we're going."

"Why, we're going to the very beginning to search for the Philosopher."

"So, we are are searching for a person!" I felt energy swell within me, inflating my groggy body. "The beginning, you say?"

"I've said too much. I must be on my way! Good day, good day!"

With a whistle and a wave, he skittered out of the bunk and into daylight's glare.

Up on the open deck, morning was busy. The skinny man swept, glaring at me as I approached. Huck clattered through a chest of bottles. Damon was kneeling down and hunched over. I felt terrible for startling him, but made no quiet approach.

"Damon! Are you sick?"

"Goodness, Fi! Try to be less quiet next time!" Something in his hand clattered to the wood.

I knelt down and picked up the object. It was a magnifying glass, its handle warm.

"What are you doing?" I asked.

"Roasting insects," he replied. "My morning assignment. Captain's already given everyone their tasks. Didn't see you in the line up this morning. Did you oversleep?"

Damon turned his attention to the crisp beetle at his feet.

"I guess I did."

From nearby, a heavy sound carried on the breeze. "Hrmph."

"Damon, I have to go. I'll see you soon," I barely got the words out. Davey was port side giving the Captain a report.

Using skills of slight I'd learned in a very short time, I moved from post to barrel, rope to bin, until I was within earshot but out of sight of Davey and the Captain.

"...that's why I think our best bet is Mundi. If we snatch some o' the puddle for ourselves, we can sell it for a pretty penny when we dock. People pay big for Mundi."

"Hrmph."

"Yea, I know about the other times, but this time we'll get it. We's got the compass and the sextants, and if tonight's stars is shinin' bright, we'll do okay. The Ursas, Perseus, Draco, all them right ones."

"Hrmph."

"Because, the ol' woman said this was the last trip out. She ain't payin' us no more after this one! You know the man's good and dead. E'ry body say there ain't no philosopher out there. Not a livin' one." Davey sniffed. "Hang on. There be a rat."

I skittered away with nothing but scraps.

VI.

Dr. Pedersen: I'd like to talk more about the childrens' father.

Freja Teuling: All right. What do you want to know?

Dr. Pedersen: We'll start slow. Tell me about the night before he left. Was it a typical evening? Were the children aware of his impending departure? Were they anxious about it?

Freja Teuling: No, they didn't know he was to leave the next morning. I'd prepared a nice dinner, and he put them to bed as usual. He told them a long bedtime story. I remember it clearly. It was one he'd made up, but it was quite good. Something about a mailman that travels to a mailbox at the end of the world. Fiona especially enjoyed it.

Dr. Pedersen: So you're saying the children were not warned of their father's leaving, and that was the last they, or you, knew of him?

Freja Teuling: Yes. That's correct. Once he left, we never heard from him again. I never learned why.

Dr. Pedersen: Do you have any assumptions? Guesses?

Freja Teuling: Knowing my husband, there could only be one reason, and that's, well, that he passed away. He loved those girls fiercely, and trust me, Doctor, if he could have come back, he would.

Dr. Pedersen: Then why the continuous search party?

Freja Teuling: Wouldn't you have done the same?

Dr. Pedersen: Yes, I suppose so.

We sit in silence before continuing.

Dr. Pedersen: On the morning of their father's departure, what were the children told?

Freja Teuling: That he had to leave.

Dr. Pedersen: But, what of the reason?

Freja Teuling: We didn't give them one. You see, Doctor, we did our best to shield the children from the reason they were homebound.

Dr. Pedersen: Please explain that.

Freja Teuling: The house was all they had ever known, so we felt that the more we kept it normal, the less likely they were to question it.

Dr. Pedersen: Mrs. Teuling, pardon my innocence in the matter, but the children were completely housebound?

Freja Teuling: I thought we had discussed this.

Dr. Pedersen: Perhaps I've been confused.

I'm thinking back to the diary about Fiona and the ship. It's not jiving with this conversation.

Dr. Pedersen: Did the girls ever visit the docks?

Freja Teuling: What? Heavens, no.

Dr. Pedersen: You had to have given them fresh air, at least in the gardens?

Freja Teuling: No.

Dr. Pedersen: Walks outside? Other schooling as they got older?

Freja Teuling: Doctor, the children suffered greatly. They wouldn't be able to tolerate it. Any exposure to sunlight would have damaged Violet's skin, and the air, I mean, her lungs...

Dr. Pedersen: What of Fiona? Why keep her housebound all her life?

Freja Teuling: Is it not obvious? I don't mean to be blunt, but you have all of her documents.

Dr. Pedersen: I want to hear your perspective.

Freja Teuling: She was dangerous, Doctor Pedersen. She didn't have the mental capability to survive in public. If I put her around strangers, who knows what would have, or could have happened.

Dr. Pedersen: What medical resources did you provide the children in the home?

Freja Teuling: The family doctor visited, but as I mentioned, my husband went in search of cures.

Dr. Pedersen: So, there was a physician for the physical ailments. What about for Fiona's mental health?

Freja Teuling: She struggled. I've told you, Doctor. That's why we kept her housebound.

Dr. Pedersen: In what ways? How did she struggle?

Freja Teuling: She could be aggressive. Manipulative. She'd see or hear or talk to things that weren't actually there or didn't truly exist. One was her stuffed animal; it was this toy fox that her father had given her. Fiona insisted it communicated with her, that it was somehow linked to her father, I think. Maybe I'm wrong in that. It was her scapegoat. As far as the aggression, she tried attacking me with a pencil to the face once, but my goodness, I could tell you stories about her antics.

Dr. Pedersen: A pencil? Why did she attack you?

Freja Teuling: Yes, a sharpened pencil. Got me good with the point of it. I remember it having to do with me washing that toy fox.

Dr. Pedersen: I'll make a note of her... tendencies. It is not atypical for someone in Fiona's position to create imaginary friends, but we can't condone violence. Mrs. Teuling, I do have one more more question before we break for today. What was the name of Captain Rasmussen's ship?

Freja Teuling: Why?

Dr. Pedersen: Completeness of notes is all.

Freja Teuling: It was called the Privateer.

45

EN ROUTE

The Mythical Vibration sat on an expanse of sea as the sun rainbowed over its decks. Its large sails were collapsed and smaller sails made ready for release. I watched from the mess hall's galley window. Eight hours passed and it felt like we hadn't moved. And yet, I'd never observed a busier crew. Even LB had been nothing more than flashes in my periphery throughout the day.

I smelled the buttery essence before she arrived.

"You seem. Perplexed."

Mykke had appeared without a sound.

"How did you...?"

"Like I. Do everything. Easily," she laughed and the sound slid down my spine.

Food sat in front of me, but I couldn't recall taking any bites. Time was flexing and relaxing in ways to which I was growing accustomed, and again, Damon's words floated through my mind. Time wasn't real, and there was only ever now.

In the now, I was missing something. I knew it like a tickle at my uvula before a harsh, chesty cold sets in. When I reached for the nagging in my throat, my mind swam like it was me that had been trying to cut through a storm, and not some alternate variation of the Mythical Vibration. It was there, this pestering purpose, and try as I might, I couldn't cough enough to bring it to the surface.

"My, my. You are. Very deep. In the thought," Mykke said.

"Why do you hide?" I asked her, not turning to face her.

"For the same. Reason as anyone. I have. Something to. Keep secret."

Gruff men populated the tables and benches around us, unshaven men with odors and cadences. I didn't ask Mykke what secret she kept, but I wondered if the opposite were true, if she was poised to run.

"Why do. You seem. So thoughtful?"

"I'm trying to figure out why I'm here," I responded.

"I can remind. You that. You left your. House for. The first time. You are. Seeing the. Entirety of. The World."

My house. It rang of an emptiness in my gut where a fullness should have been. My mind's eye conjured no concrete image.

"Yes, I think that was the impetus, but there's more. I feel like my eyes aren't truly open yet. Like, like... I'm missing something. I feel like I'm having a hard time grasping my surroundings. Like, if I knew my purpose, I'd do better here. Maybe if I knew more about the Philosopher?"

"Dear Fiona. This is. All still. So new."

"I don't think that's it." Actually, it was becoming quite old.

The grinding noise preceded his arrival. "Dinner's over. Plate here. Now." Davey's cadence didn't mimic Mykke's but instead was gritty and unkempt. He had about 15 metal plates stacked in his oversized arms as he rolled through the mess hall, seizing dinners mid-bite.

"Ye barely ate nothin' and I'd say that's waste. Ye want to know what the Capn' says about waste? No, ye don't," he spit, and I tried not to cower in his presence.

"Davey?"

"What ye want now?" It barely came out as a question.

"Can I talk to you after dinner? It's about the Philosopher."

When his eyes met mine, I was prepared for the daggers they were about to shoot.

None came.

"We arrive at Oceanus Mundi the next morn.' You want a story about the Philosopher, well, I've yet to see you earn your keep. Ain't nothin' in life given for free."

46

THE
MOTHER
RETURNS

I dreamt that night that my bed rocked with a storm's madness, that I was in a room in a white house, reaching for a bed post to steady the rocking, but steadiness would not come. Bile rose in my throat and I swallowed it down until the dream woke me and it wasn't a dream at all but the ship throwing itself around in the ocean.

"Mykke?" I cried out into the darkness.

No response came from the second bed.

"Mykke!" I yelled as I tried to stand, but the ship pitched and I fell into the wall.

Darkness swallowed the room and I felt along the wall, every notch in the wood a direction in the room's map, until I found the bedside table. The lamp was on the floor. I crawled, rolling with the heaving ship, listening for a sliding matchbox until I caught it in a pitch.

With a flick of my wrist, the room erupted in light and confirmed what I knew; we were in the throws of a massive storm. Shadows swung 180 degrees, left to right, right to left. I was a faceless figure on the wall, the ceiling, the floor, and then back again. Nausea swallowed me like a great white whale. Two seconds of confirmation, and then all was black again.

I felt my way to the door and grappled with the stairs, the railing, slipping twice. My legs ached and I kicked onward, arms holding steady until I emerged onto the top deck.

Rain pelted the ship. Men were tossed like last week's fish. The skinny man had roped himself to a mast and used the mop to push water into a bucket and the bucket turned over spilling out the water, but he uprighted the bucket and squeezed into it again.

"Fiona!" Damon's voice called to me through cutting rain.

I grabbed at something steady, but couldn't make out what it was. Spitting cold sliced into my words as I tried to call back.

"Fiona! It's her! Watch out!"

"Mykke?" I yelled through the storm.

Damon didn't answer, but no answer was needed. The ribbony arms reached up and over the side of the ship and her long hair hung in soaked strands as she climbed the side like a wiry spider.

"Give me the stone," her voice exploded over the ship. She aimed her face in my direction. "Cheater!" she demanded. "Give me the stone!"

"Fiona," Damon yelled, his voice distant. "Give The Mother what she wants! There's no other way!"

I reached deep inside of me, searching for the stone, poking at my stomach and guts, lungs and heart, extremities and head, but it wasn't there.

"Fiona! The diamond! Now!"

The she-giant rocked the ship and tossed the men. The skinny man lassoed out, hanging by his rope. Screams came from every direction as The Mother's arms whipped into sails, turning the ship into a bathtub toy.

There was no diamond inside of me. There was nothing shiny or special at all. I dove into myself then, swimming into the reaches of my fingers and toes, and came up empty.

When I resurfaced, I saw him; a shock of white, wiry hair, unconscious on the deck, his tiny body swaying with the wet debris. The Mother screamed. The Captain was nowhere.

"No," I whispered, an angry wave swelling inside of me at the sight of LB's limp body. "No."

"No," I said and took a step forward, slipping.

"No," I shouted, gaining purchase on the deck.

"No," I screamed, not knowing what I would do, but each step moving ever closer to her.

"NO," I yelled, hulking forward. And in my pocket, there it was. Not the diamond, but a graphite pencil, sharpened to a point. I knew I had to write this next moment.

"NO, NO, NO," I shrieked, grasping the pencil in my fist, lunging forward, and thrusting it into The Mother's wild eye.

47

REWRITTEN

The Mother arm's flailed for the pencil, but as it lodged in her eye, the air went out of her like a dying balloon. From the ship she fell, her ribbon arms fading into the sea. The storm died as quickly as it blew in.

I ran to where LB last lay, but his body was gone.

"LB!" I shouted, slipping in a puddle and regaining myself on a rope bundle. "LB!"

No one answered, and I realized I'd been shouting over complete stillness. More than a dozen dazed and stunned eyes focused on me until we were interrupted by one stilted, "Hrumph."

Heavy boots carried heavy legs to where we all stood. Orders were given to move sailors to their stations, reset sails, swab decks, and re-tie ropes. His gaze focused on me and I stared back, unblinking, until something tugged on my sopping skirt hem.

"LB!" I cried, breaking gaze with the Captain. I bent and hugged my small friend. "You're all right!"

"A little weary, but no more than bumps and bruises! Or is it a few bumps and bruises, but no more than a little weary?

Maybe I've conked my noggin harder than I thought. Ho ho, not to worry! It will itself right in no... right itself in no time!" LB patted at his wild hair.

"Oh, LB, I'm glad you're okay," I beamed. "Let's help you to bed."

"I can make it, dear, but thank you. You best get some rest. That was quite a show you gave us! Day's a big tomorrow... or, er, tomorrow's a big day!"

We parted ways and I crept to my cabin. Men watched as I passed among quiet cheers of "well done," and "huzzah!" and an equal earful of, "If she, uh, only given up the diamond firstly, this would ne'er uh happened."

<h1 style="text-align: center;">VII.</h1>

I'm struggling for a breakthrough in this case. More sessions pass but we are no closer to an answer than from the start. I must soon see the patient.

Dr. Pedersen: Who was allowed in the home? We haven't really discussed this. I'd like to know who was allowed to be about and around the children. Who would have had access to them and provided their daily care?

Freja Teuling: Well, it would have been myself, their father, Belinda Lally, and their full-time nanny...

Dr. Pedersen: ...and Captain Rasmussen.

Freja Teuling: Yes, I guess. I mean, it's not as though he was alone with them.

Dr. Pedersen: Ever?

She looks fearful. I've misspoken.

Freja Teuling: I, I, no. He was not alone with the girls, Doctor Pedersen. He wasn't.

I've upset her and she's doing well to control herself. A man had certainly been alone with Fiona; of that I'm sure.

Dr. Pedersen: Mrs. Teuling, what about Damon? How frequently was he with the girls?

Freja Teuling: Who?

Dr. Pedersen: Damon. Fiona's friend. I'd assume her closest friend?

Freja Teuling: I'm sorry, but there was no such person. Maybe you've been misinformed?

The journals, my notes—it's all there, Damon's name.

Dr. Pedersen: So you're saying there never was a Damon? From the docks? The ship?

She's quiet. She shakes her head.

Dr. Pedersen: What was the name of her stuffed fox?

Freja Teuling: Marlow.

Dr. Pedersen: No, I don't believe that's who I'm thinking of. You're absolutely sure she did not know a Damon?

Freja Teuling: Absolutely sure.

Dr. Pedersen: Was there ever a ship captain named Damon that you brought into the home?

Freja Teuling: Doctor, I have never in my life, not once, met a man named Damon.

Dr. Pedersen: Okay. We'll keep searching.

I write, 'no Damon.'

48

OCEANUS
MUNDI

The night hung like a thick fog. My ribs ached when I shifted, and lifting the blankets to my chin hurt my arms. I wriggled my toes. They were still there, but the movement brought deep calf aches. The Captain's glare was forefront in my mind.

"What's the danger to me today?" I asked LB from bed. The ship was motionless, but LB wavered from side to side. I rubbed my eyes to make it stop.

"Danger? Whatever do you mean?" LB had been staring at me from the cabin's door. "We're anchored at a stunning white sand isle! The sun is rising over the horizon!"

"I mean, we were almost pummeled by The Mother, so I'd like to know what I'm in for on Oceanus Mundi. Overgrown frogs? Poisonous rats? Quicksand?"

"Ho ho! No, no! Fiona, here, the danger is quite the opposite. On Oceanus Mundi, you're the danger."

"Me?" I sat, groaning. "I'm no danger. Not to anyone, LB."

"Try telling that to The Mother! You, last night, well... you were there, weren't you? With a first-hand account of the action! As for today, I don't mean specifically you, Fiona," his high pitched-voice lowered. "The danger to Mundi is humans. In general."

Dressing, I reached into my skirt pocket. The pencil was gone, proving that the night wasn't a dream. "I don't intend to hurt anyone. I never did. I don't..."

"Oh, well, yes! Don't worry yourself about that. You saved the ship! Celebrate your successes, Fiona! Now, focus. Oceanus Mundi is what's called a 'representative' island. At its heart is the Ocean, which contains all of life in itself. It's essentially the birthplace of everything that life contains, but in elemental form. The more it is explored, the more it becomes in danger of being destroyed. Despite its kindness, it does not like humans. It sees them as a threat to its very existence, so the island has a natural defense mechanism, but that defense is certainly not a danger to you."

"I beg your pardon, LB, but if an island is set on protecting itself from a creature such as me, I find it hard to believe that I'm not in danger."

"You'll see, my dear. You'll see."

When it was my turn to board the rowboat, Damon said someone had over-counted by one.

"I guess that means you'll have to sit on my lap, sweet Fi! Come now, there's no time to waste!"

I sat upon Damon and the sun was already at mid-height disc in the sky. Sweat beaded on the back of my neck and my thighs became slippery.

"Nice way to row to—" Damon was cut off.

"No boots on the island!" someone yelled from the front.

"But, our feet! They'll burn in the sand!" someone else groaned.

"The island is shaded and the sand soft as pillows," a third sailor said.

The rowboat made landfall. Water lapped at our ankles as we waded to shore, single file. At first glance, Mundi looked like every other island that could have been in any other place or book. From a sandy beach, tall palm trees extended up. In the distance, the palms became banyans, and the banyans, oaks, and the oaks, maples, and so on... until it was a forest of emeralds sparkling from its canopy.

"It has everything," I whispered, wide-eyed, stepping onto the beach.

"Does it?" LB giggled.

"What was that?" I said as silvery hair disappeared into the distance.

"Fiona, what do you think?" Damon stood behind me and outstretched his arms as if he'd created this wonder space himself.

"It's incredible, Damon. But, I'm very thirsty."

We'd stepped no more than five or ten steps and a crystal clear stream of sparkling water appeared.

"Halt!" Damon yelled. He knelt at the stream and cupped the water from his hands to his mouth. "Drink, my sweet."

The water was as refreshing as anything I'd ever put to my lips. I drank for a long time to no ill effects.

When the soft sand beneath our feet ended, the land transitioned to forgiving earth, then tender grass. No sharp stones threatened our toes. I'd never been so comfortable barefoot.

"Damon, am I floating?"

"You're walking, love. Look ahead now. There's about 100 meters left," Damon smiled.

"We've only been walking for 10 minutes," I said.

"Or ten hours," Damon replied.

"What's ahead?" I asked.

"The center of the island. The Ocean itself."

"What will we find there?"

"Fiona, are you listening? The Ocean itself!"

We marched for the last stretch, and I watched the sailors fall to their knees. I wanted so badly to rush ahead and see the Ocean, but I held my composure and stayed in the march.

The final stretch of 100 meters felt like the longest walk of my life and the island knew it. Tall firs gifted unusual fruits for our efforts and the juices flowed down my chin as I bit into the sweetest, ripest flesh I'd ever tasted.

The crowd hushed.

I came upon Oceanus Mundi.

I don't know how else to say this, so I'll state it plainly. I had no idea what I was looking at.

49

TELL ME
MORE

"Damon. Damon!"

"Shhh. Fiona, please be respectful. We're here."

Even Damon was kneeling in reverence, but I couldn't make any sense of the tiny pool that lay in the middle of more than a dozen men. There was no way that this puddle was the birthplace of all of life.

"Oh, but it is," a tiny voice buzzed behind me.

I turned and saw silvery wisps slide behind a fir tree.

Moving on my knees, I waddled backwards. "Tell me more."

Oceanus Mundi was not an ocean. It wasn't even a channel. This place was nothing more than a puddle.

"I warned you! The Ocean took itself out of danger. You knew this would happen, my dear. In fact, maybe you should take a lesson from time to time!"

"LB, I don't understand!" I tried talking from the side of my mouth so as not to disturb the quiet.

"If you want to know why the Ocean grew small,
it's really not hard to find out at all!

Simply side up to Davey and say what you seek
and 'lo and behold, the sailor will speak!"

"LB, I don't want to talk to Davey!" But he was gone, and the men were starting to rise from the puddle.

"Hrmph."

"What now?" I asked Damon

"The Captain says we're camping on the shore tonight. Mundi is allowing it."

"Hrmph."

"And that?"

"He said that since you like to talk so much, you get to be tonight's storyteller."

50

ALL OF LIFE

Oceanus Mundi provided lunch.

We collected chestnuts, coconuts, and Dungeness crabs on our walk back to the beach and dined like guests of royalty over a roaring mid-afternoon fire pit. The sun blazed but did not overheat us. Soft sand collected into drifts, gifting each of us a makeshift seat. We ate our fill until we could fit no more.

I watched Davey eat, and then I watched him lean back in his sandy cushion. I thought I watched him smile, although it may have been the curve of his lips turned upwards in a bout of gas. Either way, he seemed content. When the rest of the crew thinned from the area, I slowly made my way to him.

"Whadda you want, girl? I see you skulkin' over here," but his eyes were closed.

"I... I was hoping to speak with you about Oceanus Mundi, and maybe get some information about the Philosopher."

"I reckon' it's about time. Pull up some sand." He was neither gruff nor soft.

I sat beside him, lower than him.

"The puddle. I don't understand."

"Oh course ye' don't, but it's simple. The Oceanus Mundi protects itself from anyone visitin.' It's a great ocean that shrinks down into a puddle when approached. You saw it, but you saw it shrunken."

"Wait, that was its protective mechanism?"

"What else should it be?"

"No, I guess that makes sense. I just didn't anticipate—"

"Ye never expect, ye never think! That's the problem!"

I shrunk back.

"Go on," he said. "Ye is smarter than the crew, and I'm used to the crew."

I swallowed and continued. "We all came to Mundi, and everyone treated this puddle with complete respect. I don't understand."

"I overestimated ye. What's not to see? The size doesn't matter. All of life can be contained in an ocean or a puddle. Life is a spark and sparks ain't very big. And you only need one spark to make a life grand. A puddle is an ocean on a smaller level. What's in one is in the other and vice-a-versa."

The words floated around me, trying to find a space to settle.

Davey continued, "Whether it's the size of an ocean or the size of a puddle, it don't mean the intent for takin' care is any different. Life is life."

"And we came here, to Oceanus Mundi, to find the Philosopher?"

Davey continued, looking out over the big expanse of pink-hued sea. "It woulda made sense to find him here. Ye see, if he was looking for the source, something special, he woulda came here."

"Who is he? The Philosopher?"

"Someone a widow is paying the Captain to find. That's all you need to know."

"But, what does he want?"

"He's tryin' to learn about life. Help fix some things. That's what we think."

"Why do you call him the Philosopher?"

"Cause' he's smart. They say he's a professor."

"And this widow, she's looking for him? Because she lost him?" I'd opened the puzzle and dumped all the pieces on the floor. It was as if I could put the edges together—the flats—but couldn't see the middle.

"Aye. That's all I'll say."

"Because she still loves him?"

"Aye. Now that's enough."

We sat in silence for some time before I thought of what to ask next. The water shimmered in the distance. "Davey, did you learn anything from Mundi's puddle?"

"Aye. I learned that pretty girls talk too much. Ask another question and ye better run!"

VIII.

Dr. Pedersen: Fiona on the day of her first major sedation... tell me about that.

Freja Teuling: Well, let's be clear. Fiona was sedated fairly frequently. But on the day of the first major one, we fought her to the bed. The doctor injected her with a sedative into her arm vein, the one here.

She gestures to the bend in her elbow.

Freja Teuling: He shone his light into her eyes to make sure it was working. At one point, her body reacted much like a seizure, and the doctor inserted a wad of bedclothes into her mouth to make sure she wouldn't bite her tongue off. When she began to choke, he pulled it back.

Dr. Pedersen: What prompted this first sedation?

Freja Teuling: Violet had an accident and Fiona reacted extremely poorly, almost out of control.

Dr. Pedersen: What type of accident?

Freja Teuling: Violet fell down the main stairs in her wheeled chair and became concussive. It was the first of a series of significant medical downfalls.

Dr. Pedersen: Your family doctor sedated Fiona as a reaction to Violet's accident? Why? For how long?

Freja Teuling: We had to. Fiona was out of control with hysteria. Doctor, when Fiona raged, she was destructive. So, she was sedate for about a week. The medicine gave her fits of hot and cold spells, she fell off the bed, had to be bound more than once. I believe she even seized a few times. She'd shriek and scream, and yell things that made no sense. It was difficult, but her physician said it was common with the medication she was on.

Dr. Pedersen: Was Mr. Rasmussen present during this week? Or was he at sea?

The room is silent for a moment.

Freja Teuling: Why do you ask?

Dr. Pedersen: Mrs. Teuling, I'm simply trying to get a sense of all accounted for.

There is no sense in expounding on my suspicions now. The woman is brimming with guilt.

Freja Teuling: Yes. I mean, he was in the home.

Dr. Pedersen: Mrs. Teuling, did Fiona have, let's see, how do I want to put this... a reclusive place?

Freja Teuling: I'm not sure I understand. She had her bedroom.

Dr. Pedersen: Perhaps. It could be a room in the house, it could be a person in which she confided; I mean, we are aware of the stuffed fox and her journals. Well, now that I think out loud, maybe we've established that she couldn't have gone far.

Freja Teuling: She had her bedroom.

I wait, but the woman says no more.

Dr. Pedersen: Let me try to ask this in a different way. When Fiona was upset—when she was more than upset—when she became irrational, had these outbursts, needed the sedative, was there anything consistent about her behavior? We have a tendency to call these consistencies 'coping mechanisms.'

Freja Teuling: I'm trying to recall... it was always so hard to tell with her. Clearly, you could see that she wrote copious amounts in her journals. She became a ferocious writer, especially in her later years.

Dr. Pedersen: Perhaps her reclusive state was in her own words... in her own head.

[Silence.]

Dr. Pedersen: You've told me about her behavioral inconsistencies. What else did she exhibit?

Freja Teuling: You know, she would mumble about trees. She had a preoccupation with trees, and she always seemed to turn, I don't know, inward, after her episodes. She'd talk about the trees, but it would be incoherent. I couldn't tell you what it meant.

I annotate the word 'trees.'

Dr. Pedersen: Because she was not allowed outside and had never been outside. She likely longed for nature.

Freja Teuling: The house was locked from the inside.

Dr. Pedersen: And this sedation you described earlier, this was Fiona's last sedation?

Freja Teuling: No. The last sedation was by far the worst.

Tears fill the woman's eyes.

Freja Teuling: The absolute worst.

51

FEEDING
TIME

"What are they doing, Damon?" I asked, watching Huck and some of the others collect sticks into a giant pile.

"Oh, my love, I'm so proud of you!" He clapped his hands, then cupped them to my face. His eyes were giant orbs in the moonlight. "They're getting the night ready for your story. My love, the storyteller!"

My stomach sunk into my bottom. I had completely forgotten. "A story? Oh, no. I can't Damon. I don't have any stories."

Damon held my face. Again, he spoke with a gentle touch but a fierce tone. "I'm not sure you assess the situation correctly, sweet Fi. You weren't given a choice."

I paced the beach while men built a fire. Accessing the stories in my brain seemed like opening a blank journal.

"LB," I whispered, "are you around?"

No silvery tufts glittered near the beach.

"LB, I could really use a friend."

"No, you could really use a story, ho ho!"

The tinny voice entered my ears from several directions at once.

"Where are you?"

"Trying to help you find a story! And, I think I've got it!"

"How? I can't remember any." The more I considered this, the more sweat beaded at my neck on this cool, breezy evening.

"You were previously passed hundreds, if not thousands of stories from someone who loved you, Fi-O-Na. They were entrusted to you and then you entrusted them to your own writings. Simply open one of your books in the attic of your mind. You'll find a story there."

The voice disappeared.

A story entered.

I walked to the beach, where are roaring fire and word-starved men waited to feast.

And I fed them.

52

THE MAILBOX AT THE END OF THE WORLD, PART 1

I began by clearing my throat. The men eagerly waited. I focused on the roaring fire and not the two dozen or so eyes boring down upon me.

"There once was a postman who was given the worst assignment in the history of the Post. It was the service that no men, nor women, wanted to perform, and the unlucky winner was pulled once a year from a central postal repository of all postal names from around the world." I looked around to make sure everyone was listening. Most eyes were on me, and Damon's were glistening in the soft light. I took a deep breath and continued.

"In fact, this event was so despicable, so hated, and yet," I paused, "such a great honor, that the winner was announced on Christmas Eve over the royal airwaves from Denmark, the United Kingdom, the United States, I mean, by the President of the United States..." Looking around to see if anyone had caught my slight falter, I saw that the crowd had settled and all eyes were mine.

Standing, I moved closer to the crowd. It was the first time I could smell them, and though they looked like sweat and drippings, they smelled like pineapple and dessert. "On Christmas Eve, with their bellies full of plum pudding, all the postmen and postwomen of the world gathered round their radios in the warmth of their homes and waited while a bag full of names was shuffled.

This particular year, the person that would be serving the greatest honor for the entire worldwide postal society sat in his living room, mourning the loss of his family only a year earlier. As he sipped his tea with lemon, he waited, unaware that his name was the one that was about to be announced around the world.

'David Verne, congratulations,' the Queen of England held the honor this year. 'You are the postman that will spending your year delivering the post to the Mailbox at the End of the World.'

Somewhere over the airwaves and seated in his living room, David Verne dropped his teacup, spilling its contents all over his newly polished hardwood floors."

53

THE MAILBOX AT THE END OF THE WORLD, PART 2

"Fi, you're doing fabulously! Look at their eyes - they are shining for you, my little diamond. Keep going," Damon whispered in my ear and then melted back into the night-time crowd.

The fire continued to burn, higher and brighter than before. "On the first of January, David Verne waved goodbye to his parents and the few friends that had come to see him off. His boat was filled with the trip's necessary supplies; the boat itself a small wooden thing, stacked to unreal heights with food, water, clothing, pillows and blankets, stationary, and a single framed photo of David's deceased family. It had been his only packed sentiment.

Though comically stacked to the sky with goods, when David shoved off, the oars cut through the water like a hot knife through butter. Landward goodbyes carried on the wind. David glided backwards, rowing as if he carried no weight at all.

On day one, David Verne felt light and happy. He'd opened his canned peaches, heated a hot cocoa on a small flame, and sang himself to sleep with sea shanties as the dingy rocked him into dream. Day two brought journaling and a pencil sketch of the horizon.

On day 45, he cried and blasphemed the Queen's name, shouting and waving his arms toward the heavens and wishing he'd never become a postman at all.

Day 129 was the day he took his knife, held it against his throat, blunt side only, and cut. He cut and hacked at the length of beard that had grown down his chin. After that, he'd felt a somewhat refreshed man again.

As the sun peered its edge over the horizon on the hundred and eightieth day, David Verne and all of his newly acquired rowing bulk saw a dilapidated mailbox appear on a small patch of land in the distance.

The man was so overwhelmed that he'd arrived, so overjoyed, that he stood in the little wooden boat, flung his arms to the sky, and almost tipped the entire operation. Settling back quickly and regaining his composure, he lowered his voice. Instead of shouting 'hooray,' he whispered, 'hooray,' for his throat was dry as sand, and maneuvered the boat to land.

When the boat was safely lodged in the sandy patch of land, David stepped out, feeling the jelly legs he'd come to expect. Land wavered below him, and each step felt like he was walking on a plump marshmallow.

David Verne took his postal bag from the boat, jelly-stepped all the way to the mailbox, the VERY ONE AT THE END OF THE WORLD..."

I'd stopped then and looked around. Night had settled in, and every set of eyes burned with reflected fire and the mounting tension of my story.

"...and stood before it before falling to his knees in a prayerful reverence. Tears streamed from his face because he was able to fulfill this once-in-lifetime duty, to pick up the mail from this faraway wonder. He took the photo of his family, almost two years deceased now, and showed them. This was all for them. A shaking began in his core and spread to his fingers as he reached for the mailbox. David felt as if there should be a sense of ceremony to this event, the opening of the mailbox at the end of the world for the first time in a very long time, but in the absence of a great idea, he simply waved his arms around, looking a bit like a flailing... um, magician."

Someone in the audience coughed.

"His fingertips touched the mailbox, and he thought he felt them burn with excitement. Sliding the lid open, he found..."

"WHAT DID HE FIND?" a voice boomed from the crowd.

"He found that the mailbox was empty."

"ARE YE KIDDING ME?"

Someone shushed the man in the back.

"David dropped to his knees and cried and cried. Tears streamed from his eyes to his mouth, tasting of the sea. Then, the idea struck, and he rushed to his boat, grabbed his pen and stationary, and sat and wrote. He wrote about his family, about their untimely death in the accident, and about how he believed it all lead to this very moment. The pen transcribed it all. David's life came out in a torrent of waves; about how, perhaps, if there had been a letter in the box at all, he wouldn't have the opportunity now to write out his grief, to tell his story, and let his heart breathe.

'If the next person to open this mailbox reads this and takes anything from this, it's hold your loved ones tight, don't be wrought by grief, and live life to the fullest.'

With a flick of his tongue, David sealed the envelope, and left it unmarked. He placed the envelope in the mailbox at the end of the world and left it for the next person to find.

Then, he rowed away."

54

THE MAILBOX AT THE END OF THE WORLD, PART 3

I continued, "After another 180 days, David Verne made landfall with the announcement that the mailbox was empty. All over the news, it was printed, 'POSTMAN'S FAILURE,' as papers reported his year-long misadventure.

'I must go back,' he announced to the Postmaster General, who relayed his message to the Queen of England, Denmark's Royal Family, and the President of the United States of America. 'I volunteer to return again.' All over the world, he was lauded a hero for saving another postman from having to take the trip.

'WHY?' The newsprint headlines read.

David Verne had to know who responded to his letter. He, and only he, had to be the one to see the response with his own eyes.

The boat was repacked, and with more food, because David carried more muscle than ever before from all of his rowing. This second trip, he rowed so fast, he made it to the mailbox at the end of the world in 134 days. Practically collapsing onto land, he crawled to the mailbox at the end of the world, shakily opened the lid, and cried to see a letter in the box."

"WHAT DID IT SAY?" someone yelled.

"David took the letter from the box to find that this letter was unmarked, and a bit weather-worn. It was thick, as if someone had taken care to write pages of story. A shaking crept throughout his fingers first, then his wrists, until he felt the rumble through his heart, which shot down to his toes.

Carefully, he unsealed the envelope's edges. A series of pages fluttered in his hands. The words that began the lonely letter read: 'Dear Reader, Despite my disappointment at arriving to find this mailbox empty, I've recovered quickly at this prompt realization: had there been a letter in this box, I would not have had this opportunity...'

The first page fluttered from David's hands, and then the familiar second, and third, until his own words carried on the wind and sea, and the mailbox was once again empty. David, too, stood empty until once again filled with resolve that came from an invisible inside tank. Hands shaking from rowing sores, he wrote another letter much like the first, sealed the envelope with as much spittle as his mouth could muster, and enclosed it within the mailbox. This time, the box would hold a letter, and this time, it was up to someone else to find it.

David's lesson was one in perseverance, even when it appeared that the whole of England was against him. He understood that now. With peace in his heart, less paper in his boat, and no return letter to speak of, he made his way home, to carry on."

The mens' eyes were large, and each set stared at my face. For minutes, no one spoke.

"It's the end of the story," I said, unsure of myself.

"The Philosopher," one whispered from the back. I could barely hear him.

"The Philosopher," another said, a little louder.

"The Philosopher," one from the front whispered. He stood, but did not move.

It went on like that until they'd all taken a turn with the words. Then, I heard the sound. Familiar and uncomfortable, but I'd known it anywhere: boots that swished with water. I looked at him, trying to locate his eyes, but only a foreboding shadowy figure loomed before me in the evening light, a man two-times his normal bulk in the fire's projection.

"The Philosopher," the Captain said aloud, the boom projecting out from the ghastly dark. Those were the only two words I would ever hear him speak.

Heat rose from my face and chest.

Damon stepped forward and put his arms around my waist, moving hair from my face. He kissed my cheek. "No," he declared, and with a smile, hoisted me up onto his shoulders. "No," he said louder, with a triumphant rise to his voice. "The Philosopher's daughter."

IX.

Dr. Pedersen: Between sedations, Fiona remained roomed with Violet?

Freja Teuling: The girls remained in their childhood bedroom until the last day.

Dr. Pedersen: You trusted Fiona alone with Violet after the first staircase incident?

Freja Teuling: Dr. Pedersen, Fiona wasn't involved in that incident. I mean, she and Violet tussled, but it's not like she pushed Violet down the stairs. Besides, I always believed that Fiona's vigor was what kept Violet going all of these years. What Fiona maintained in physical health, Violet maintained in mental health. And what Violet lost in physical health, Fiona lost in mental health. They balanced each other. Could you have separated two such twins?

Dr. Pedersen: I see your point. And when you say, 'until the last day,' what exactly do you mean by that?

Freja Teuling: Until Violet's passing.

She is crying again.

Dr. Pedersen: Do you wish to discuss that now?

Freja Teuling: Will there ever be a good time?

Dr Pedersen: Mrs. Teuling, please, when you're ready. There's no rush.

Freja Teuling: Fiona was getting older. Almost nineteen years by that point, if I recall. Perhaps already nineteen. Speaking to inanimate objects with increasing regularity, as if they were her friends. Violet was rapidly declining, often bed-bound, and our family physician felt that Fiona was acting out in response.

Dr. Pedersen: Does this make any sense in that context?

I hand her an open diary.

Freja Teuling: '*Water, water, make me not hear, blind, deaf, dumb blind. Gills, breath through gills? Choke?*' I can't make heads or tails of this. This is what she was like around this time. Nonsensical.

Dr. Pedersen: Well, that's what we are here to sort. What happened in particular that prompted the final sedation?

Freja Teuling: I left the girls alone one afternoon. It was a Sunday. The journal may confirm that. Well, who knows if poor Fiona could even tell her days back then. I hadn't heard any noise from their bedroom in sometime, so I went upstairs to check, and thank goodness I did.

She resumes after a moment.

Freja Teuling: Doctor Pedersen, it was horrible. I opened the bedroom door and found Fiona holding Violet over an open second-story window. Heavens knows how she even wrenched it open. That window had been sealed shut for their safety. Fiona didn't respond to the sounds of my shrieks. She was repeating, 'fly, little birdie, fly. Go on now, fly,' or something to that effect, in this hushed voice. I couldn't snap her out of it. I crept up behind her and brought the two of them crashing back on the floor.

She shakes violently, recounting these events. I reach out a hand and the woman recoils.

Dr. Pedersen: Apologies, ma'am.

Freja Teuling: That was the day.

Dr. Pedersen: Which day?

Freja Teuling: The last day that Violet ever held consciousness. The doctor said she experienced a brain bleed when she hit the floor.

We sit in silence for several minutes while the gravity of the situation fills the room.

Dr. Pedersen: Mrs. Teuling, this is not your fault. Look at me.

When Freja Teuling looks up next, her eyes take on a muted color. She is the embodiment of someone completely different. This Freja Teuling is colder.

Freja Teuling: When you meet my daughter, remember all of this. Fiona's sickness is such that she'll lie to you, and you'll believe it.

Dr. Pedersen: I'm sure I will be able to tease out the truth.

She shakes her head.

Freja Teuling: I lived for nineteen years believing that Violet was safe from her own sister. If she speaks to you, you'll believe anything she tells you, Doctor Pedersen. Every word.

Dr. Pedersen: Mrs. Teuling, I have one more question for you. Did Fiona ever wish to leave the house?

Freja Teuling: Every single day of her life.

55

THE
DAUGHTER'S
RETURN

After the men had their rowdy fill and tired themselves for the evening, Damon lay with me in the sand recounting my story's bits and pieces. Ocean crashed nearby and swished in my ears. I was woozily tired, having a hard time discerning fact from the pull of sleep.

"I still cannot believe we had you with us all along," Damon's voice swirled with my head on his chest. "Where did you read that story?"

"I didn't read it. It's a legend," I told him. "Legends aren't stories contained in books."

"All this time, we sought the Philosopher, but we knew—we knew!—he's been gone for ages, stories of his ship wrecked at sea, and our clue..." he laughed. "Our only clue, but we thought we'd had it wrong."

Against my failing eyelids, visions flashed. *A father with two daughters. Stories. A white home. Footsteps. 11:34. Spit.*

"Damon," I said, gasping. "It's all wrong."

"Yes! The bird! When you came on board, the bird uttered a word."

"The bird?" I repeated, eyes now wide.

"Yes, the Captain's bird. It uttered a word, the only word any of us remember hearing it speak. It said, 'sister.'"

"Sister," I trembled.

Damon smiled. "Well, that's what we thought, but the bird... it's never spoken before. When silence speaks, don't you listen?"

Closets. Fox. Pudding. Attic. Books. Corners. Floors.

"I don't know..."

"Well, you're the Philosopher's daughter, so how about you solve the puzzle? The rest of us cannot, other than it's obvious that you're her."

Sand shook underneath me.

"You're thinking, I can hear it," Damon said. "Your thoughts are so magical, they hum."

The sound grew louder, closer, but only when it was practically on top of us did I hear this noise:

hrmph.

Hrmph.

Hrmph.

It was the Captain walking with Davey, and I saw only a flash of them before the sack was tossed over my head, and someone big and strong heaved me over his shoulder and carried me away, kicking and screaming.

56

CAUGHT

Darkness.

I'd fought against darkness until my limbs went limp.

Davey said nothing as I kicked against his chest and punched into his back, but I was exhausted and gasping for air. I wasn't sure how long had passed until I stopped moving and focused on breathing, letting my burning lungs readjust to the sack that inhaled against my lips with each breath.

Sounds changed from the evening's hum to wood clanging against wood for a long while, to the deafening silence of being in an enclosed space. Through the sack, I could smell it, the staleness of the ship's interior, and something else, something feral.

Hands reached for me and I fell hard on my backside, hard onto a wooden surface, hearing the grind of metal against metal. Then, stillness. Stillness on a keeling ship.

Slowly, I moved my hands and removed the sack from my body. It had never been tied.

My palms bled from pressed fingernails and thrown punches.

My toes ached from kicks landed in boots.

Knees, elbows, stomach hurt from being bent over a wide shoulder, and my head... oh, the room spun.

It hurt me, the man's touch.

Then, I heard it, or, I think I heard it. I don't think I could have seen the single lost feather fall to the floor, not in this darkness. But when my eyes adjusted, cabin darkness lightened. I was alone in a cell of locked wooden bars.

Perched on a stand was the bird: a bundle of matted and thinned feathers clinging to an emaciated clawed creature. I'd once thought the creature all black, but I could now see, even in the dimness of the room, that the feathers reflected a purplish hue, those feathers the color of a deep bruise.

That smell. Bedroom. Window pane. Channel. Surge.

I scrambled to my feet and to the edge of the cell, my hands outstretched for the bird.

The bird refused at first, said nothing, did nothing.

My hand was only inches from its perch, but I could not reach, no matter how hard I stretched.

"Please," I cried. "Please, please." Sobs wracked my body and an ocean opened up from my face. My arm dropped to my side. "Please," I pleaded, knowing I was bound to drown.

Papa.

And when the sea of tears rose high enough to meet the bird on the perch, the bird floated towards me. We were at eye-level, this bird and myself, with this ocean I'd created. It looked right at me.

As tide receded, the bird never shifted its gaze. When the tide was gone and the room was dry again, the bird nestled in my lap, coughing, coughing, and I rubbed its bony back, trying to soothe its body.

Its cough was like baby fingernails, trying to scratch my own throat.

I petted its head.

"Cough, cough," it cried.

"It's all right. You're safe. You're dry," I said. "I'm sorry. I'm sorry. I'm sorry."

The bird coughed so hard that something flew from its withered, broken beak. I watched it skid across the floor, mucus-covered and black.

A key.

My arm shot through the bars of the cell, hand reaching for the object, but struggle as I did, the key fell inches out of reach.

"Please," I cried to the bird, "please, can you push it near me?"

I set the small body on its feet outside of the cage and watched it take one step, two steps, and then collapse from the effort.

"No," I whispered, panic rising in my throat, "wake up. You're okay, you're okay!" I paced the cage like a frantic animal.

Noise approached from outside of the cell room and I retreated to the corner.

Minutes passed, but it may have been hours. There was no more day and night, but only time.

Breaths became seconds, but I couldn't keep count. Exhaustion was a deep sea. I watched the bird breathe.

I knew something in that moment: I would die in this cage.

57

UNLOCKED

I don't know how long I'd slept before her hands touched my shoulders, and my battered body screamed as she sat me upright.

"Fiona you. Must stay. Quiet."

"Ow, it hurts," I pleaded.

"I know," she whispered. "But I'm here. To get. You out."

"Violet," I began, first feeling pain in my head, and then in my arm, and my legs, one pain at a time until my body was registering the fiery locations across its own map, node by node.

"She is. Back with. The Captain."

Mykke placed her arms around me and gingerly put mine around her neck. I held tightly, burying my face in her skin.

"The Captain! We'll be caught. Mykke, you can't take me out of here." Sobs escaped my lips, but I didn't fight her as she stepped into the fresher air outside the cell room.

"My father. Would do. No such. Thing. Not when. I threatened. To tell. Who my. Mother is. You are. Safe now."

58

UNMOORING

"We are. Returning home."

Home.

The word felt hollow and uneasy.

"Mykke?" I struggled from a parched throat. We were locked in our cabin, but I felt like a storm took hold of my insides. My lips trembled.

"Calm now. You are experiencing. The return. We are. Flipping back."

She rubbed my hair, allowing the waves in my face to settle.

"Who are you?" I managed. "I mean, what is your story?"

"Yes, yes. You may know," Mykke breathed in and held it for a moment. "I am. The daughter. Of the Captain. and The Mother."

"From the Equaaga tribe?" I heard it leave my lips as "ee-aaaaaaaa," but Mykke understood.

"Yes."

"Why do you never leave the ship?"

"The Captain. Hides me. I am. Both worlds. His abomination. So I stay. Hidden."

A volcano boiled from my insides threatening to erupt from my vocal cords, but I remained quiet. I fumed at the thought of the Captain's beautiful daughter a ship captive.

"Mykke, you are the goodness that came from their darkness. You deserve more. You deserve better."

She continued to rub my hair with her smooth fingers.

"Fiona, how. Do you. Cut down. Darkness?"

I opened my mouth to speak, but all that came out was one weak squawk.

59

DOORS

Mykke left and I gave in to exhaustion until the rough sea demanded that I come above board for air. The process of flipping back shook my insides and my insides swirled into the sea.

"Look at me," the sea demanded as I hung over the side of the ship.

I kept my eyes closed.

"Look at me," she insisted, and I could not ignore her demands as I was in her and she was in me.

"Mama?" I called out.

The sea did not respond.

For the first time, I yearned for this place of home. Eyes opened, I stared down. The sea became glass.

Home.

A house.

A smell.

A room.

A window.

A reflection stared back at me, and I winced, an inherent fear of something hurtling my way swam to my surface; an ancient, inbred reflex.

There she appeared, my mirror image. Purple, scrawny, sunken eyes. Beak-like nose. Hunched shoulders. Ravaged hair; a tangle stuck across my lips. Birdlike fingers reached up to release it from the drool that tightly clung to it. Sulfurous water sprayed back into my nostrils, and I smelled the face: the face in this swirly, watery, unclear mirror.

It was time to go home.

But, I had one last thing to do.

I had a door to break down.

X.

Captain door open.

You expecting me. Round window.

Each step, he grew smaller.

SQUAWK!

EXCUSE ME!

Captain didn't move. Left bird cage open empty. Slosh slosh.

Not weight. I Float.

Captain shrink.

WHAT A TERRIBLE SMELL!

Window OPENS!

Window eyes are a mirror.

Violet flies out. BE FREE! I TOLD PAPA YOU'RE FREE! HE MADE ME PROMISE!

Fiona wins. Captain is nothing. NOTHING! VIOLET ALL BETTER!

Can't breathe, can't breathe, can't breathe. Can't breathe, can't breathe, can't brrr—

60

CAPTAIN'S QUARTERS

The Captain's door was open.

"You were expecting me." It wasn't a question. I hardly posed it to him as he sat in a straight-backed chair staring out a round porthole.

"Hrumph." He didn't move from the chair, nor did he turn to face me.

The clock in the corner showed 11:33.

Farther into the room I ventured and with each step forward, the Captain grew smaller.

"Squaaaaaawk," a voice called out.

"Excuse me?" I asked.

The Captain didn't move. I looked to my left and saw a littered birdcage, open and empty. I stepped closer, slow and measured. With each step, I began to hear her slosh inside of my shoes. She was not weight. No; she was buoyancy. As the Captain shrank, I grew, and still, he refused to look.

When I neared him, his familiar dirty smell invaded my nostrils. I unlatched the porthole with ease and the window popped open. Had his eyes met mine, I would have seen it there, his reflected intention. It was not the same as mine, but its reverse.

It took one, two, and then a third beat of her wings, and out the round window the purple bird flew.

"You're free, little bird," I cried. "Be free, little bird."

Caws cut through the atmosphere as she struggled against the wind.

"Free!" I screamed through the tiny window. "I promised him," I sobbed. "Papa, she's FREE!"

I looked back and saw the Captain shrinking to nothing. The room shrunk around me. I carried the weight of water in my boots, and the sea was inside me and I was the sea. The sound of ocean flooded my ears.

Water, water everywhere, and its noise was deafening. Water, in my ears, my eyes, my nose. I reached up under my hair and felt for my gills.

They were nowhere to be found. I began to choke.

INTERLUDE

Freja Teuling heats a modest lunch in her kitchen. A pot of stew leftover from the previous day's dinner simmers on the stovetop. She turns up the flame and takes a gentle sip off a ladle. The spice rack to her right holds rosemary, which she grabs, slowly removes the lid, and adds a pinch to the pot.

Everything Freja Teuling does these days is slow and deliberate. Time has taken on a new meaning, but only in a sense of the word. Freja Teuling has yet to put action to meaning. She's waiting on her weekly delivery of fish, now a small and modest order as she is only one in a once large household.

Staring into the small pot, a bubbling stew captures her attention, holding it hostage as her brain drifts elsewhere. Her hand grips the rosemary jar.

The front door's bell rings.

Freja Teuling turns down the heat and walks toward the door to greet the day man and his small and modest fish delivery.

The day man, with his fresh delivery.

"Delicious, Mama. From the docks?" Fiona chewed.

"A new delivery boy. Said he's from the docks. He brought a sampling by the house on the cart after school today."

"What did he look like?"

"Fiona," I warned her. "Inappropriate."

The day man.

Day-mon.

Damon.

She drops the rosemary jar to the ground and it shatters on uneven floorboards.

XI.

Dr. Pedersen: Welcome. Please, have a seat.

The woman appears younger than her stated age of twenty-one years. Her hair is neatly plaited in two rows down her back and tied with bows at the ends. She wears a simple dress of cotton, sensible shoes, and carries a small stuffed toy animal that may be a dog or a fox. It has no eyes. The animal appears well-loved and dirtied.

The woman sits in the same seat her mother sat in, and doesn't speak when I approach with simple questions, like name, general likes, or even minor conversation about the weather.

I continue to push forward with questions, which are met with stares, at times blank, at others dark, and at once, pleading.

XII.

We try again the next day.

XIII.

We try again the next day. The young woman doesn't acknowl-edge the tea I hold in front of her.

XIV.

On the fourth day, I turn her chair to face the office's picture window. The curtains are spread wide, and I've provided her with a view of the icy channel below. Although her view of me is obscured, I am able to observe her in profile. I attempt conversation again, patient with the woman. I have experienced this type of mutism before and it is often the result of trauma.

At the window, the woman's shoulder's relax. The dog-fox falls to the side of the chair, and she stares intently at the world outside; the water, perhaps.

Dr. Pedersen: Fiona. Welcome. I'd very much like for us to be friends and get to know each other.

The woman leans forward, lips are slightly apart. I lean forward, listening, but still no sound escapes.

Dr. Pedersen: Fiona, I know you've been to a few doctors, but I don't want you to think of me that way. In fact, I think of you as a writer. I've read your work, and I'm quite fascinated by it. I'd rather you think of me as a collector of stories, and you the storyteller.

I wait for several minutes.

A flock of dark birds is returning from an early migration. Fiona's eyes are fixated on them. She reaches for the window, for the birds, I think. A frayed piece of string hangs from her wrist.

Dr. Pedersen: Yes, I think it would be nice if you could take the role of storyteller, and me, the story collector. Then, you could come here daily and speak, and I could sit and listen like a child in wonder! I could ask questions and help you tell a great tale!

The approach seems to pull her attention from the birds.

A cracked whisper escape her lips.

Dr. Pedersen: Yes?

Another whisper.

Dr. Pedersen: Go on... I can almost hear you.

Her voice breaks and sound rushes out.

Fiona Teuling: Children passed outside.

[*She whispers. I walk to the office window but no one passes below. Hallucination?*]

Fiona Teuling: ...walking to the real schoolhouse with books under their arms, skipping and laughing while my faced pressed against the cool bedroom pane. Behind them the channel surged, swollen with its late fall overflow. I didn't dare break my gaze. One boy caught my stare and threw a pebble at the window. It bounced where my face pressed. It was him, the same wicked boy that threw rocks into the channel.

She doesn't look at me. While her voice grows slightly louder, there is no pitch change, no tone to her voice. It is flat, except for the word 'wicked,' upon which she places emphasis.

Dr. Pedersen: Please, continue...

Fiona Teuling: I didn't blink.

Dr. Pedersen: Did the boy say anything when he threw the rock at the window?

Fiona Teuling: 'Take that, Violet!' His yell was muffled by the glass plate. They never got our names right, no matter how many times I mouthed them. Violet was so sickly, small, and blue: two rainbow shades off from her namesake. The boy stopped and stared at me, dead in his tracks, like Papa used to say.

Dr. Pedersen: And how did you respond?

Fiona Teuling: I didn't blink.

Dr. Pedersen: Yes, but what happened next?

Fiona Teuling: [*Mimicking another voice*] 'Oh, children can be wicked. Fiona, step away from the window 'fore you catch cold.'

Dr. Pedersen: What was happening in that moment, Fiona?

Fiona Teuling: Nanny was remaking my bed.

Dr. Pedersen: What did you think of that?

Fiona Teuling: I already made the bed. Tight corners, for a ten-year old.

Dr. Pedersen: Where was Violet during this scenario?

She continues to stare out the window.

Fiona: Violet sat in her chair at the table. Violet—

Dr. Pedersen: And—

I've accidentally interrupted her. She doesn't appear to mind, but I worry it may change the course of the conversation. She is looking at me, but I cannot read her eyes. They appear empty, lifeless. We have some work ahead of us.

Fiona Teuling: —less than ideal company.

Fiona Teuling: A door slammed down the hall. Heavy boots passed our bedroom. Nanny pulled at the bedding and I wanted to scream at her to let it go.

Her voice rises. This is likely enough for today.

Fiona Teuling: [*Mimicking another voice*] 'Ms. Lally will be here soon, girls.'

She turns and stares at the outside world.

Dr. Pedersen: What did you do next?

A long pause follows.

Fiona Teuling: I withheld the scream.

ABOUT THE AUTHOR

Annie James Thomas is the pen name for Kimberly Pesaturo, a New England-based writer, mother, and educator. She is a co-founder of Loud Coffee Press.